The dream had felt so *real*

As Jenna padded to her bedroom, the dream hung around her like a cocoon, images flitting in and out, vague and muddled, but that desperate feeling of wanting, needing made her ache.

The harder she tried to remember the dream, the more it evaded her. But she could almost still feel *him*. His presence, his touch, his essence.

"Sexual frustration," she said with a laugh. Her laugh sounded hollow even to her own ears.

The warmth of him, lying in his arms, his touch arousing her in ways—

She stopped, staring down at the bed. Her body turned to ice. Her heart began to pound erratically.

There were two impressions in the down-covered mattress. One on her side where she slept. The other where someone else had lain next to her.

B.J. DANIELS
WHEN TWILIGHT COMES

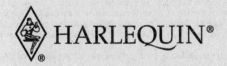

HARLEQUIN®

TORONTO • NEW YORK • LONDON
AMSTERDAM • PARIS • SYDNEY • HAMBURG
STOCKHOLM • ATHENS • TOKYO • MILAN • MADRID
PRAGUE • WARSAW • BUDAPEST • AUCKLAND

When I decided to become a writer I just wanted to tell stories. I'd never met a writer, knew nothing about the business or the blessings that come with it. One of the greatest gifts I have realized is the friendship of other writers. This book is dedicated to two of the best: Amanda Stevens and Joanna Wayne.

ISBN 0-373-22876-7

WHEN TWILIGHT COMES

www.eHarlequin.com

Printed in U.S.A.

ABOUT THE AUTHOR

A former award-winning journalist, B.J. Daniels had thirty-six short stories published before her first romantic suspense, *Odd Man Out,* came out in 1995. Her book *Premeditated Marriage* won *Romantic Times* Best Intrigue award for 2002 and she received a Career Achievement Award for Romantic Suspense. B.J. lives in Montana with her husband, Parker, three springer spaniels, Zoey, Scout and Spot, and a temperamental tomcat named Jeff. She is a member of Kiss of Death, the Bozeman Writer's Group and Romance Writers of America. When she isn't writing, she snowboards in the winter and camps, water-skis and plays tennis in the summer. To contact her, write: P.O. Box 183, Bozeman, MT 59771 or look for her online at: www.bjdaniels.com.

Books by B.J. Daniels

HARLEQUIN INTRIGUE

*Cascades Concealed
†McCalls' Montana

CAST OF CHARACTERS

Jenna Dante—Is it just an accident that she ended up at the isolated hotel at the end of the road while running to protect her daughter?

Lexi Dante—Jenna's precocious four-year-old.

Harry Ballantine—The con man has one chance to make up for his past. But he didn't count on that chance involving a woman like Jenna Dante.

Lorenzo Dante—No one took from him and lived to tell about it. Especially his ex-wife, Jenna.

Raymond Valencia—The crime boss broke his cardinal rule—he got involved with the wrong woman.

Rose Garcia—She thought she had her life under control.... That was before Fernhaven.

Charlene Palmer—She knew the value of friendship.

Chapter One

Jenna Dante ran her fingers down the cold steel barrel of the gun in her jacket pocket as she parked in the darkest part of the estate.

Through the trees, she stared at the second floor bedroom window, willing the light to go out.

It took everything in her to wait another twenty minutes after it finally did so. Then she picked up the crowbar from the seat next to her and, making sure the dome light was turned off, slipped from the car.

Because she would be carrying a heavy load when she left, she'd taken the service road, parking at the back entry closest to the house.

The hired help had gone home hours ago. Lorenzo didn't like anyone staying on the estate at night. That was because he didn't want any witnesses.

The gun weighed down her pocket as she moved stealthily through the trees and darkness toward the servants' entry. She'd worn all black, and had picked this entrance because it was the farthest from the main part of the house.

At the door she pulled out the ring of keys, thinking she would have to use the crowbar. But the key she chose fit in the back door lock and turned. She stared down at it, surprised that she could still be shocked by Lorenzo's arrogance. He'd been so sure she would never use her keys that he hadn't even bothered to have the locks changed?

Or was he expecting her?

She froze, her pulse drumming in her ears.

With the crowbar in one hand, she turned the knob and pushed open the door. He hadn't reset the security system when he'd come home, either.

She felt a chill race up her spine as she stood in the rear entryway, fighting to calm her nerves. Desperation had brought her here. Desperation and anger. She drew on the anger now, reminding herself of everything Lorenzo Dante had done to her. He had taken her dignity, her innocence, her confidence. He'd hurt her every way possible. But this time he'd gone too far. This time he'd taken the one thing she couldn't let him get away with, no matter what happened here tonight.

She stood listening for a moment, then slowly closed the door and put down the crowbar. The arrogance that had kept him from changing the locks and turning on the security system would be his downfall, she told herself. Better to believe that than consider he didn't even see her as a threat.

The thought brought a fresh surge of anger. She needed it desperately if she hoped to succeed. Fear was a weakness, one she couldn't afford. Not tonight. But anyone who didn't fear Lorenzo Dante was a fool, and Jenna was no longer a fool.

Cautiously she crept up the stairs to the second floor. The carpet was soft and deep, her footsteps silent. She stopped near the top. She could hear music playing in the living room. Classical music. Lorenzo must be in one of his moods. He tried to forget his humble beginnings by pretending he was a man of breeding.

But during their marriage, Jenna had noticed that he played classical music when he was trying to convince himself he was somebody, that he wasn't just some thug who'd made a lot of money illegally, that he didn't have enemies who were more powerful than he was.

Tonight he must be feeling vulnerable.

The thought surprised and scared her. He was more dangerous when he was like this. She wondered why he was in this mood. He should have been on top of the world. After all, he'd struck another blow against her, one that he knew would destroy her.

Something was going on, she realized. Something to do with the business? Or her?

At the top of the stairs she looked down the long hallway. The door to the room she was most interested in was closed. Her fingers itched to open it and slip inside.

But first she had to know where Lorenzo was.

She pulled the gun from her pocket and crept down the hall, noticing that the door to the master bedroom was open.

Another piece of music came on. Over it, she heard the rattle of ice cubes in fine crystal. She felt another jolt of concern. Lorenzo was making himself a drink? Something was definitely going on.

Moving silently along the thick carpet, she crept to the landing at the top of the stairs that overlooked the living room. She gripped the gun tighter in her hand as she held her breath and peeked over the railing.

Lorenzo stood in front of the fireplace with his

back to her. He held a drink in his hand, his gaze apparently on the fire, an anxious set to his shoulders.

He was a large man. Just the thought of his big hands on her made her stomach roil. Her finger skittered over the trigger of the gun as she raised it and sighted down the barrel, pointing it right where his heart should have been.

You can't kill him. Not in cold blood.

She wasn't so sure about that. Not after five years with Lorenzo. Not after everything he'd done to her.

She thought about him turning and seeing her, seeing the gun. She could imagine the smirk on his face, could imagine him taunting her. He wouldn't believe she could kill him.

Even with a gun in her hand, he wouldn't see her as a threat. He thought he knew her so well, figured she would be too afraid to come after what he'd taken from her.

But she also knew him. Maybe better than he knew her. She knew his one weakness: arrogance. He'd been so brazen to come back here—to not even try to hide from her. Because he had the courts and the police where he wanted them. Jenna had learned the hard way that she couldn't beat him through the system.

And because of that, he thought he had Jenna where he wanted her, as well. That was her edge. That's why she had to move fast.

She lowered the gun, sliding it back into her jacket pocket, and turning, stole down the hallway again. As she started past the master bedroom, she noticed once more that the door was open. Lorenzo's suit jacket was lying across the bed. She slipped into the room and moved to the nightstand on Lorenzo's side.

Reaching into the space behind the table, her fingers brushed across duct tape and cold steel. She ripped Lorenzo's gun off the back of the stand and peeled the sticky tape from the grip.

She didn't need to check if it was fully loaded; she knew it was. Lorenzo was meticulous about that sort of thing. But she looked, anyway. Tonight she wasn't taking any chances.

The gun *was* loaded. She slid the safety off with a soft click. Pointed it at the open doorway, slipping her finger through the guard, caressing the trigger, getting the feel of the larger, heavier piece.

Then she lowered the gun, snapped the safety back on and stuck the weapon into the waistband of her black jeans, so it was covered by the tail of her jacket.

As she started to leave the room, she saw something that stopped her cold. When Lorenzo had thrown his suit jacket on the bed, something had fallen from the pocket. At first all she saw were the passports.

With trembling fingers she picked up the top one and saw Lorenzo's photograph, but with an entirely different name.

She began to shake harder as she picked up the second passport and opened it. Tears of fury sprang to her eyes at the sight of the photograph.

Bastard. He was planning to skip the country. That's what was up. That's why he was feeling vulnerable tonight. His "associates" must not know his plans, because Lorenzo belonged to an organization that knew only one type of retirement program: death.

Unless he had made some kind of deal to buy his way out.

But the passports weren't the only things that had been in his jacket pocket, she saw. She pulled out two airline tickets and had to steady herself when she saw the date Lorenzo had booked for a one-way flight to South America. *Tomorrow.*

Shaking furiously, she ripped up the tickets and threw them into the wastebasket beside the bed. Then she pocketed both passports and hurried down the hallway to the smaller bedroom. As she opened the door, she could see the slight rounded shape under the covers in the glow of the night-light. Her heart lodged in her throat at the sight of her sleeping child.

Jenna eased the door closed behind her and tried to stop shaking, angrily fighting back tears.

She moved quickly to her daughter's side. She couldn't let Lexi see her anger. Or her fear.

The silky dark hair was spread out on the pillow, the little face that of a cherub. Lexi had one arm around her beloved rag doll, Clarice. The other was looped around the neck of her cat, Fred.

Fred looked up as Jenna stepped deeper into the room, and let out a loud meow.

Jenna hurried to the baby monitor and shut it off.

Fred blinked at her with huge golden eyes.

"Lexi," she whispered as she knelt over the bed. "Wake up, sweetie."

Lexi's lashes fluttered, then suddenly flew open. Her dark eyes widened in surprise. "Mommy? Daddy wouldn't let me see you." Her lower lip pushed out into a pout. "He said you had gone away."

Jenna hushed her. "It's you and me who are going away, sweetie. But it's a secret. We have to be very quiet, okay?"

Lexi nodded and threw back the covers as she sat up. She was wearing the little yellow ducks pj's Jenna had bought her. The same ones she'd been wearing last night, when Lorenzo had broken into her apartment and taken Lexi.

"I need you to be very quiet," Jenna told her daughter. "We don't want to wake up Daddy."

Lexi nodded and put a chubby finger to her lips. "Shh."

Jenna picked up her daughter, hugging her tightly as she breathed in the sweet smell. Lexi felt solid in her arms. Safe. At least for the moment.

"Come on," Jenna whispered. "Remember, we have to be really quiet, okay?"

Lexi nodded, clutching her rag doll. "Is Daddy coming with us?" she asked in a small voice.

Jenna looked at her daughter's face. "No." She saw the instant relief and her heart broke. "Did Daddy hurt you?"

The child shook her head, her lower lip pushed out again. "He yelled and made me cry."

Jenna hugged her. "Well, he won't make you cry again." She stepped to the door of her daughter's bedroom and started to open it.

"Fred!" Lexi cried. "I can't leave Fred."

Jenna groaned inwardly. She'd never been a big fan of cats. Lorenzo had bought the kitten for

Lexi, knowing Jenna wasn't allowed to have a cat in the apartment where she'd been living with Lexi since the divorce.

"Alexandria will have to come over to the house to see her cat," Lorenzo had said.

Which meant Jenna would have to come as well, since Lorenzo only had supervised visitation. He'd gotten the cat to force Jenna back to the estate—a place she had grown to abhor.

Now she stepped back into the room and, with her free hand, picked up Fred from the bed. He complained loudly as she hooked him into the crook of her arm.

She waited until he settled down before she opened the bedroom door and glanced down the hall. Empty. She could still hear the classical music.

She crept along the back hall, then down the stairs. She was almost to the back door when she heard an approaching car coming up the service road. Was it possible Lorenzo had called for a delivery this late at night?

Moving to the window, Jenna peered out as headlights flashed. The whine of an engine rose, then died as the car pulled in directly behind hers.

No! Whoever it was had blocked her car in.

The police? Or some private patrol?

But as she peered through the blinds, she saw

that it was one of Lorenzo's "associates" who climbed out.

Franco Benito. He looked toward the house, making her step back and let the blind knock against the window frame.

She moved quickly down the hallway, stepping into the laundry room and partially closing the door. Motioning to Lexi to be quiet, she held both her daughter and the cat as the back door opened. Franco closed the door a little more forcefully than usual. She pressed herself and Lexi against the wall as the man stormed past. She caught only a glimpse of him, but he looked angry. Probably because Lorenzo had made him come to the service entry. Why had he done that?

She breathed a sigh of relief as Franco's heavy footfalls fell silent.

How was she going to get away now, though? He'd blocked her in. And what if he mentioned her car to Lorenzo? Lorenzo would know she was in the house—and he would know exactly what she'd come for.

LORENZO DANTE FINISHED his drink and poured himself another as he tried to calm down. He glanced at the clock on the mantel, checking it against his watch.

Nine fifty-seven. Franco was twenty-seven minutes late. He hated people who weren't punctual. People who made him wait.

He gripped the glass, anger seething inside him as he looked around the country estate, reminded of all he had accomplished—and how little respect he'd garnered. He deserved to be treated better than this. Because Franco was taking his place in the organization, did he think he didn't have to treat him with respect? The glass shattered as he crushed it in his hand. Blood ran down his wrist and dripped to the floor.

Lorenzo stared at it in surprise, having forgotten he was even holding a glass. Opening his hand, he let the pieces tinkle to the Spanish tiles.

Two shards were stuck in his palm. With a kind of distracted fascination, he plucked them out, dropping them to the floor as he watched fresh blood run from the cuts down his wrist.

He turned at the sound of footfalls behind him. "You're late."

Franco Benito stopped in the middle of the floor, clearly startled by the sight of the blood and the broken wineglass.

Lorenzo smiled as he stepped to the bar and leisurely wrapped a wet cloth around his hand, all the time keeping his gaze on Franco, considering the best way to teach the two-bit thug respect for his betters—and the value of being on time.

"I'd take a drink if you haven't broken all the glasses," Franco said, clearly irritated himself.

Lorenzo smiled at the idiot's attempt at humor. Franco hadn't liked being ordered to come through the service entry. Too bad.

Without being offered a drink, Franco stepped to the bar beside Lorenzo. Franco was a good-looking guy, not really big, but strong. His one great flaw was that, because he was taking Lorenzo's place in the organization, he thought Lorenzo was powerless against him.

Franco was so clueless. He reached behind the bar and wrapped his thick fingers around the neck of an expensive bottle of bourbon. Taking a glass—the wrong kind for bourbon—he sloshed some of the amber liquid into the expensive crystal with arrogant abandon, spilling enough fine liquor on the bar to make Lorenzo wince.

Franco turned to face him, raising his glass in a mock salute. After drinking it down, he sighed and smacked his lips, smiling at Lorenzo, almost daring him to comment as he reached for the bottle to pour himself another. After tonight, Lorenzo wouldn't have any power in the organization. And Franco would.

But the night wasn't over.

Lorenzo grabbed the back of Franco's neck and slammed his face down on the bar, into the spilled booze. He heard the thug's nose break like a twig even over the howl of pain.

"Shut up. You'll wake my daughter," Lorenzo snapped as blood poured from Franco's nose, a stream of bright red.

Franco staggered as he let go of the bourbon bottle and fumbled for his weapon.

Lorenzo could feel himself losing control, and tried to pull back as he snatched the bourbon bottle off the bar and brought it down sharply, dropping the thug to his knees. It would have been so easy to finish him right there and then.

Franco had his gun in his hand, trying to find the trigger through the blood pouring down his face. With a swiftness born of survival in the dog-eat-dog, violent world Lorenzo lived in, he reached behind the bar and came up with the sawed-off shotgun.

Jamming the end of the barrel against Franco's temple, he brushed his finger lightly over the double triggers as he met the man's gaze. It was all Lorenzo could do to restrain himself. If he didn't, he would definitely waken Alexandria.

Franco glared at him, clearly caught between

an irrational desire for retribution and the need to stay alive.

Lorenzo watched the ignorant thug weigh his options, and smiled to himself when Franco slowly dropped his gun to the floor.

"What the hell is wrong with you?" he demanded as Lorenzo lowered the shotgun. The thug plopped into a sitting position and leaned back against the bar to cup his hand over his broken nose. "Are you crazy?"

Lorenzo put the shotgun back behind the bar and poured himself another drink, glad he hadn't pulled the trigger. It wouldn't have just awakened his daughter, who was sleeping upstairs, it would have added to his problems with their boss, Valencia.

After tonight, though, Lorenzo would be free of Valencia. All he had to do was keep his cool, get the money he owed Valencia and give it to Franco. Just a few more minutes and it would all be over. He would have bought his way out of the organization and would soon be on a plane to another country. A new life. What did he care if Franco was acting too cocky? Or if Valencia was determined to stay legit now and thought he could run things without him? Let Franco try to take his place.

Lorenzo downed his drink. He unwrapped his hand and tossed the bloody bar cloth on the floor next to Franco. "Clean yourself up while I check to make sure you didn't wake my daughter."

"Just get the money." Franco glared up at him, then angled a look at his gun, lying on the floor within reach.

Lorenzo cut him a smile. "You'll get the money. If you live that long."

Franco gingerly picked up the bar rag and held it to his nose, leaning his head back, closing his eyes—disappointing Lorenzo by not going for the gun. "Valencia isn't going to like this."

Lorenzo considered kicking the thug, but feared he wouldn't be able to stop once he started. He walked past him, his expensive Italian shoe brushing Franco's calf, making the man draw his legs up and open his eyes. Lorenzo was rewarded by the fear he saw shining there. Maybe Franco wasn't as stupid as he'd thought.

But Franco was right about one thing: Valencia wouldn't be happy about this. Lorenzo didn't know what had gotten into him. He'd never liked Franco, never trusted him, and he sure as hell didn't like the idea that Valencia had picked Franco to take his place in the organization. Lorenzo didn't like what it said about him that Valencia thought someone like Franco could replace him.

As Lorenzo climbed the stairs to Alexandria's room, he felt his blood pressure start to come down, along with his temper. By tomorrow he would be on his way to a new life. No more Francos. No more Valencias.

And to make his new life even sweeter, he would have his daughter with him. He smiled at the thought of his ex-wife and how much pain that would cause her. Jenna deserved much worse. It would be all he could do to leave the country without killing her first. But he took pleasure in knowing Jenna would die a slow death just knowing he had Lexi, and that she would never see her daughter again.

At the top of the stairs, he glanced down the hallway, immediately on alert. The door to Alexandria's bedroom was partially open. He was positive he'd closed it earlier. Had she gotten up for some reason? She'd been upset earlier, wanting to see her mother. He'd had to spank her to get her to quit asking for Jenna. Was it possible she'd run away, thinking she could find her way to that awful apartment Jenna had rented after the divorce?

Or had someone taken Alexandria?

His step quickened as he told himself he had to be wrong. But even before he grabbed the doorknob and turned it, he knew.

As soon as Jenna was fairly sure that Franco wasn't coming right back out to his car, she pushed open the laundry room door, sneaked down the hall and slipped out the rear door of the estate. She knew she wouldn't get far on foot carrying Lexi and the cat.

"Mommy?" Lexi whispered. "I'm cold."

"I know, baby. Hang on." The child was growing heavy. The cat started to squirm. Jenna knew she couldn't put Fred down. He might run off. She had to do something and fast.

She glanced toward the four-car garage. What choice did she have? She'd have to take one of Lorenzo's vehicles.

But when she opened the side door she saw that the garage was nearly empty. Lorenzo had sold all but one car: his large black SUV.

Of course he would have sold the cars. Because he was planning to leave the country. She should have known. He'd been too calm during the divorce, too agreeable. True, she hadn't asked him for anything but Lexi. Still, it hadn't been like Lorenzo to give up anything that he felt was his. He'd never planned to let her get away with Lexi.

Jenna stared at the large black SUV. Lorenzo always left his keys in it, as if daring anyone to steal it. Her heart leaped at the sight of Lexi's car seat in the back. Did she dare?

The ridiculousness of the question made her laugh. Lorenzo was going to kill her for stealing Lexi back. It wouldn't matter what else Jenna took.

She opened the rear door, set Lexi in her seat and Fred on the floor. The cat jumped up on the back sat beside Lexi as Jenna snapped the child in, before rushing around to the driver's side and slipping behind the wheel.

Once she opened the garage door, she would have to move fast. She reached for the key.

LORENZO DANTE LET OUT a howl of anger and pain at the sight of the empty bed, the covers thrown back, Alexandria gone.

He couldn't believe what he was seeing. He glanced around, checked the bathroom, ran down the hall to his bedroom. No little girl.

Letting out a string of curses, he charged into his daughter's room and ripped the covers from the bed, whirling them into the air in a rage as he crushed the fabric in his fists the way he would crush his ex-wife's throat when he found her.

It had to have been Jenna who took the child. Part of him still couldn't believe it, though. Jenna knew what he would do to her. She was smart enough to fear him. He'd made sure of that as soon as they were married. He'd gotten her young so he could train her to be the wife he wanted. She'd bent to his wishes from the start, because she'd had no other choice.

Until Alexandria had been born a year later.

That's when Jenna had started to change, he realized now. The pregnancy hadn't been her idea. In fact, he was almost certain she was entertaining thoughts of leaving him when he'd decided to change her mind by getting her pregnant. Foolish young woman that she'd been. As if he had ever planned to let her leave him.

She'd thought he didn't know about the birth control pills she had started secretly taking. He'd simply replaced the contraceptives with sugar pills, and was pleased when she'd quickly gotten pregnant.

He'd thought he had her exactly where he wanted her. Now she would obey him. Now that she was tied down with a baby. And it had worked for a while. He'd tried to act the loving husband and father.

But he'd learned the hard way that she, too, had

been acting. He'd come home one day to find her gone. She'd filed for divorce, gotten a restraining order against him. She couldn't have thought he would ever allow her to leave him, let alone take his daughter.

Unfortunately, he'd gotten into some trouble inside the organization and needed to keep a low profile. At Valencia's urging, Lorenzo hadn't fought the divorce. He'd let Jenna think she'd gotten away with it—and sole custody of Alexandria. He'd even let Valencia think he wasn't going to cause Jenna any trouble.

But no one walked away from Lorenzo Dante. No one took anything of his, either—and lived to tell about it.

Jenna had stolen his daughter. First in court, then again tonight. Just because he'd let her think she'd gotten away with it the first time, now she thought she could do it again? He blamed Valencia for tying his hands and keeping him from taking care of Jenna right away. If he had killed her the moment she'd taken Lexi and filed for divorce, he would have saved himself a lot of aggravation.

He flung the blankets back onto the empty bed, wanting to trash the room to relieve the anger that had started building downstairs with just the thought of seeing Franco tonight. Then Franco had been late....

Lorenzo reminded himself that the thug was still downstairs. Waiting.

It would be impolite to make him wait, Lorenzo thought with grim humor.

Wanting to finish his business with Franco so he could deal with his ex-wife, Lorenzo started out of the room, then heard a car engine.

He ran to the window and looked out in time to see his black SUV come tearing out of the garage. In the glow of the garage light, he saw Jenna behind the wheel. She'd taken his car, too?

Fury tore through his veins like a grass fire in a stiff wind. What did she think she was doing?

He started to charge out of the bedroom after her, already thinking he could take one of the other cars, chase her down, run her off the road and—

He stopped as he remembered. He'd sold the other cars because he was skipping the country. Just as he'd sold the house and everything in it. Because he planned to fly out as soon as he settled up here tonight. He didn't want any hired killers coming after him. That's why he was buying his way out of the organization.

The realization that he wouldn't be able to catch her hit him like a blow. He'd made Franco come to the service entry to show contempt for him and his new job. Even if he took Franco's car, he wouldn't be able to catch Jenna. She was on an entirely different road, was getting away, and there was nothing he could do about it.

He slammed his fist into the wall three times in quick succession. Franco called up an inquiry, which Lorenzo ignored as he tried to calm down.

That's when he remembered. All the air rushed out of him. The money. The money to pay off Valencia. He'd left it in a duffel bag in the back of the SUV.

No! He felt his knees go weak. He had to sit down on the edge of the bed to keep from falling. The room blurred in a haze of red as his rage sent his blood pressure soaring. His money.

No, not *his* money. *Valencia's* money. As if taking his money wasn't bad enough, she'd taken the money he owed a man who could crush him— and would.

He'd kill her. If Valencia didn't kill him first. Lorenzo swore and dropped his head into his hands. He'd never dreamed Jenna would come to the house and try to take Alexandria. She knew what would happen if she did. What the hell was wrong with her? The woman he'd married had been so shy and quiet, so submissive, so malleable.

Even during the divorce, Jenna hadn't asked for a penny of his money in court, refusing even child support when the judge had tried to insist on it.

So what had happened to that woman? A woman who would never have taken his daughter, let alone his damn car, and worse, his money.

He pushed himself to his feet. He couldn't call in his stolen car to the cops. Not with the money in the back. Nor could he send the cops after Jenna for taking their daughter. She had sole custody. Not that he'd ever put much store in handling things legally, anyway.

His hands began to shake.

He would get the money back. That wasn't the problem. The problem was Valencia. Unfortunately, Valencia expected the money *tonight*. It was the reason Franco was waiting downstairs. Franco and his broken nose.

Lorenzo's mind raced. Valencia wouldn't believe that the money had just gone missing. Even if Lorenzo told him the truth—that Jenna had taken it along with Alexandria—Valencia wouldn't cut him any slack.

No, the boss would be furious that Lorenzo had taken Alexandria. Valencia had ordered him not to fight the divorce, not to seek retribution. That bastard had never even shown any sympathy for what

Lorenzo had been going through with Jenna. It was one of the reasons Lorenzo had decided to secretly take his daughter, settle up with the organization and leave the country. And there had been a couple of previous disagreements over money with Valencia that had already caused some bad blood between them.

Lorenzo didn't need this.

Valencia had been willing to let him walk away from the business, from the past. But now Lorenzo might be considered a liability, someone who knew too much and couldn't be trusted, and therefore was expendable. Valencia might feel forced to kill him.

For an instant Lorenzo thought about just taking off, skipping the country tonight, running for his life. He had a passport in a new name and enough money hidden around the country to live on for some time.

He pushed himself off the bed and hurried down the hall to his bedroom. He reached behind the nightstand on his side of the bed, instantly realizing the weapon he kept hidden there was gone.

His gaze fell on his suit jacket. He grabbed it up, knowing before he searched the pockets that the tickets and passports were gone, as well.

He wrung the garment in his hands, wanting

desperately to rip it to shreds. But even before he'd found the passports missing, Lorenzo knew he wasn't leaving the country.

Valencia would hunt him down like a rabid dog. Plus, Lorenzo knew that just the thought of Jenna getting away with not only his daughter, but also all that money, would drive him insane.

He swallowed back the bile that rose in his throat. No, he would have to stall for time until he could get the money back. But he would get it back. The money *and* his daughter. He could always get new plane tickets, new passports.

But he couldn't leave without making his ex-wife regret ever being born.

"Hey?" Franco called from downstairs. "Hey! Valencia's waiting for his money. He's going to be pissed enough when he sees my face."

Lorenzo nodded to himself in the empty bedroom. Franco had a good point. Valencia wouldn't be happy on either count.

As he left the room, Lorenzo stopped at one of the heating grates, pried it open and took out another of the weapons he kept hidden in the house—one that even his dear wife hadn't known about. He shoved the gun into the small of his back and descended the stairs.

Franco never knew what hit him.

Chapter Two

Jenna Dante had been driving for hours through the pouring rain and darkness when she came around a corner in the narrow road.

She couldn't believe what she was seeing. Water. It tumbled down the hillside from a rain-swollen creek, flooding the road ahead. The raging water ran over the highway and on down the mountainside like a river.

She slammed on the brakes, her fingers gripping the wheel. The SUV began to skid on the wet pavement, directly toward the deep water flowing onto the highway.

She wasn't going to stop in time, and once she hit the moving water…

She cranked the wheel, felt the SUV begin to spin out of control. *Lexi!* It was her only thought as the car crashed into the side of the mountain.

There was a terrible sound of metal ripping, then silence.

For a moment, Jenna couldn't move. Her gaze shot to the car seat in the back. Lexi was awake and looking at her. "Are you all right?" Jenna cried.

"What happened, Mommy?"

"We just went off the road. It's all right." She peeled her fingers from the steering wheel, shaking so hard she had to grip her hands together in her lap. "But we're fine." They were fine. Her air bag hadn't even deployed. But she could hear the water rushing by not feet from them. They wouldn't be fine for long.

The car engine was still running. She shifted into reverse, praying that the car wasn't damaged badly, that she could drive out of here.

But the moment she pressed on the gas pedal, she realized they weren't going anywhere. Not in this car.

She shut off the engine and unhooked her seat belt. The rain seemed to have lessened as she climbed into the back and hurriedly got her daughter out of her car seat. Grabbing her purse, Jenna opened the door and climbed out, reaching back to lift Lexi and her rag doll in her arms.

"Fred!" Lexi cried, and grabbed for the cat.

"I'll come back for him," Jenna promised. But Lexi already had a death grip on the animal, so it looked as if they were all going.

Jenna wasn't even sure where they were. Somewhere in the Cascade Mountains. All she knew was that she hadn't seen a house or another car for miles.

"Mommy? Clarice is scared," Lexi whispered, one arm around the rag doll and Fred, the other squeezing tighter around Jenna's neck.

Jenna tried not to let her own fear immobilize her. The car was wrecked. They were out in the middle of nowhere. And Lorenzo would be coming after them. Could already be after them.

Fred let out a loud meow in her ear, as if agreeing with the rag doll. It was definitely scary.

"Clarice shouldn't be afraid," Jenna said. "She has you to make sure nothing happens to her. And you have me."

Right. She felt her stomach clench with fear at just the thought of how helpless she was against Lorenzo. But she had Lexi. And Lorenzo would take her again over Jenna's dead body.

She almost laughed at the truth in that. She never wanted to see him again and didn't think she probably would. He never did any of his own dirty work. Of course, this time he might make an exception. He would want to kill her with his own bare hands.

She shivered at the pleasure he would derive from it.

Jenna walked back up the road, away from the raging creek, trying to decide what to do. She had few options. The road was blocked, might even be washed out by morning.

Not that Jenna was going anywhere in the SUV. From what she could tell, the car was high centered on a rock. Or worse.

The rain had almost stopped. Fog rose from the pavement, and beyond that was nothing but darkness.

She tried her cell phone. No service.

Out here she felt so vulnerable. But they couldn't have stayed in the car—not with the water so close and possibly still rising.

She half expected to see car lights coming up the road. Half expected Lorenzo to be behind the wheel. Could just imagine the expression on his face. *Gotcha!*

In the weeks since the divorce, she'd often wondered why he'd let her go so easily. But in her heart she'd always known. He wanted her to think she'd gotten away. Gotten away with her daughter. When in truth, it was just a cat-and-mouse game with Lorenzo. He'd known that he could end it in an instant when he was ready.

Had he taken Lexi knowing Jenna would come after her? Had he just been looking for a reason to come after her and kill her? Not that he needed one.

She shuddered, telling herself that nothing could change the course of events. And if she'd never married him, she wouldn't have Lexi.

Jenna's heart broke at the thought that she might not be able to protect Lexi from her father. It had been a last resort, taking her back from Lorenzo the way she had. Now she couldn't let her daughter down. No matter what she had to do, she thought. Shifting the cat she reached for the gun still in her jacket pocket.

"Lookee!" Lexi angled a tiny finger out into the darkness beside the road.

Jenna had to crane her neck to see where she was pointing. Lights glowed from out of the fog. High up on the side of the mountain she could make out the top spires of a building poking up out of the trees and mist.

And there on the hillside was a sign, barely visible in the gloom. The neon outline of a woman in an old-fashioned bathing suit, in a diving pose. Underneath her, the words Fernhaven Grand Opening. The date on the sign was in three weeks.

There was definitely something up the road—a huge building, the lights glowing faintly through the swirling mist.

"I want to go there!" Lexi cried. "Please, Mommy? Clarice wants to, too. She said she wouldn't be scared at all if we went there."

"I don't think it's open yet," Jenna said. Whatever it was. "But we'll go see."

As she moved forward, the glow of lights high on the mountainside became clearer. No wonder she hadn't noticed them earlier from the highway.

If she could get her daughter somewhere warm and dry, she could call for a wrecker. They just needed someplace to wait. It had to be close to midnight by now.

The freshly paved road wound up the mountain. They hadn't gone far when she had to put Lexi down and catch her breath. After that, the child insisted on walking. Thankfully Jenna had grabbed a sweater for her daughter. She put it over the footed duck pj's. Jenna carried Fred, but Lexi wouldn't give up her rag doll, Clarice. The going was slow, the darkness around them intense. Along the road the trees were dense and dark.

Jenna was beginning to think this was a mistake when they crested a hill and the road abruptly widened. There, shrouded in fog, was a huge castlelike building looming out of the night.

She couldn't contain the chill that moved over her.

Fred dug his claws into her arm, seconding Jenna's thoughts. This place gave her the creeps, too.

"It's a castle," Lexi cried.

If this was a castle, then an evil count lived here, Jenna thought. But then, she'd been living with evil for some time. She still wondered how she could have been so deceived by Lorenzo. Why hadn't she seen what kind of man he was before she'd married him? She knew the answer. Lorenzo was very adept at hiding his true nature. But living with him, she'd quickly seen through his facade right down to his black soul.

As tired as she was, she wouldn't have been surprised if the hotel turned out to be a mirage. But all the lights were on in the huge lobby, and she could see someone inside.

"Come on, Mommy," Lexi said, and ran toward the wide front steps.

The air was damp and cold. Jenna could hear a roar as if there was a waterfall nearby. She caught up to Lexi, taking her hand. As they ascended the wide steps, Jenna looked up.

The face of a man appeared at one of the third-floor windows. She had the distinct impression he'd been watching them as if waiting for them. Maybe the hotel was open to guests, after all.

She had little more than an impression of him before he was gone.

HARRY BALLANTINE WASN'T sure what had made him go to the window and look out. Just a feeling.

Even more odd was what he saw from the window: a slight-framed woman with a young child, and something in her arms. A cat.

So what had drawn him to the window after all these years?

Apparently the woman.

She was dressed all in black, her dark hair pulled back in a ponytail. She wore no jewelry of any great value, something he could tell even from this distance. Her face, pale in the foggy light emanating from the lobby, had the appearance of both strain and exhaustion, but also fear.

She was in trouble. Why else would she be banging on the door of a not-yet-opened hotel after midnight on a rainy night?

He saw no reason why he might be interested in her. In fact, there was every reason not to get involved in whatever trouble she was in, even if he could help her.

That's what made it so strange. He *was* interested. Something had drawn him to the window. Just as it now drew him to the woman. What worried him was that he had no idea why.

RAYMOND VALENCIA CALLED Lorenzo just before midnight. "What the hell?" he said by way of greeting.

Lorenzo had gone to bed, turning out all the lights, just as he would have if nothing unusual had happened tonight.

"Raymond?" he asked, pretending he'd been awakened from a sound sleep. He sat up, fumbling with the lamp beside the bed. "What time is it?"

"Where the hell is Franco?"

"Franco?" He yawned. "How should I know where Franco is?"

"You might recall he was at your place to pick up something of mine a few hours ago," Valencia snapped. "Or don't you know anything about that, either?"

"Actually, he was late. Didn't get here until almost ten, seemed…nervous. Smelled like he'd been drinking."

There was silence on the other end of the line.

It was all Lorenzo could do to keep from filling the space, but talking too much would only make Valencia suspicious.

"What time did he leave with the money?"

"Right away," Lorenzo said. "I offered him a drink, but he said he was in a hurry."

More silence. He could almost hear the wheels in Valencia's head turning. Franco was a man Valencia trusted so much he was going to let him take Lorenzo's place. And Franco knew firsthand what happened to anyone who crossed the boss. It was no wonder Valencia was having a hard time believing that Franco would betray him.

"He probably stopped off to see his girlfriend and lost track of time," Lorenzo said, yawning again. "Hell, he probably had a fight with her and that's why he was late and had been drinking. Women. They can twist a man up good."

"What girlfriend?" Valencia demanded. "I know nothing about a girlfriend."

"Oh yeah?" He shrugged, counted slowly to five. "I don't know her name. I just overheard him on his cell with her one day. She was giving him a hard time, from the sound of it. He was kissing her butt, trying to calm her down. Pretty funny, really."

Valencia swore. Even a man as cold and hard

as Raymond Valencia knew the effect a woman could have on a man.

Lorenzo smiled to himself when Valencia slammed down the phone without another word.

He'd offered the bait and the boss had taken it. Lorenzo put the receiver back in its cradle and turned out the light, lying in the darkness, thinking about the way Jenna had messed him up.

His first impulse was to go after her. But he couldn't indulge that impulse. If he left town now, Valencia would become suspicious. More suspicious than he no doubt already was.

No, Lorenzo had been forced to put one of his former employees on Jenna's trail.

He'd called a man who was so dumb Lorenzo trusted him. Alfredo made Franco look like a genius. The man was all brawn and no brain, and because of that he was like a robot when it came to just doing his job without any questions. Alfredo didn't even complain about being awakened in the middle of the night. He said he would find Lorenzo's ex, not let anyone know where he'd gone, and "detain" her until Lorenzo could join them at a later time.

"Good. I want to handle this myself when the time is right," Lorenzo had said.

"No problem."

He'd hung up. He hated waiting, and here he was going to have to wait some more. But he had confidence that Alfredo would find her and the money, and that was all that mattered. As long as it was soon.

The problem was what to do once he had Jenna and his daughter and the duffel full of money. Maybe he would just tell Valencia the truth. Valencia would be furious at him for killing Franco, but Lorenzo figured it was something he could get over. Especially since Valencia would have his money back.

Or…Lorenzo could go with plan B. He could keep the money, take his kid and get out of Dodge. By then Valencia would be fairly convinced that Franco had ripped him off. Lorenzo could maybe plant some evidence, a trail for Valencia to follow that would make it even clearer that Franco had taken the money. Franco and his girlfriend.

What if Franco really did have a girlfriend? Lorenzo had had to lie about overhearing Franco on the cell phone with someone. But what if the stupid thug really *did* have a girlfriend? That could mess things up good.

Lorenzo swore, almost wishing he hadn't killed Franco. If Franco had a girlfriend, then Lorenzo would have to find her before Valencia did.

Chapter Three

Jenna followed Lexi up the steps and across the hotel's wide veranda, then knocked on the door. Earlier she'd seen someone moving around inside the expansive lobby, where several huge ornate chandeliers glowed brightly.

Lexi peered in, seeming enchanted by the place. It was definitely elegant, from what Jenna could see. Expensive, too. And apparently not open yet. Had she just imagined someone inside earlier? What about the man she'd seen at the third-floor window?

She pounded harder.

An elderly man appeared from out of the back. He seemed surprised to see her.

"We're not open for business yet," he called through the glass.

"My car went off the road down by the creek," she called back. "The road is flooded. We just need somewhere to stay until I can phone for a wrecker."

He held up a finger to signal he would be right back. Good to his word, he returned with a key and opened the door. "Sorry. Come on in. The road's out?"

She nodded, and she and Lexi stepped in. The moment she entered she felt a brush of cold air move past her cheek. She shivered as she looked around. "What is this place?"

"Fernhaven Hotel. The exact replica of the one built in 1936."

That explained why the place had the feeling of another time. The lobby was huge, with massive planters of ferns and palms, rich fabric-covered sofas and chairs, Oriental rugs spread over hardwood and marble floors that gleamed. The crystal chandeliers sparkled. Through high arches she could see thick burgundy carpet running to the elaborate entrance of a huge ballroom.

"Nothing was quite like Fernhaven at the time," the elderly man said. "I remember my parents talking about the place. It opened during the Depression, but there were still some that had money and wanted to be with other folks with money in someplace isolated. Couldn't get more isolated than this," he said with a laugh.

"Do you have a phone I could use? I tried my cell phone but it doesn't seem to work up here."

"Sorry, didn't mean to talk so much. Gets lonely up here." He was tall and whip thin, with a shock of gray hair and thick brows like caterpillars over pale eyes. "You're welcome to use the phone in the office, but I doubt you'll be able to get anyone out tonight. The closest town is to the east, and if the road is flooded… Give me a minute. I should call the highway patrol first, so they can put up a roadblock at the creek."

He left her and Lexi, and went into the back. Jenna could hear him on the phone. When he returned he said, "The creek isn't the only stream flooding tonight. Sounds like there's more problems on the road you came in on. I'm afraid you're not going anywhere for a while." He glanced from her to Lexi.

Jenna realized what they must look like. Though the rain had stopped, there was enough moisture in the air to make them both damp and chilled.

"I can put you in a room for the rest of the night," he offered. "We're not officially open, but we have some suites on the third floor that are finished." He waved off her concern. "The rooms are just sitting up there."

She had no choice, she thought, gazing at her daughter. Lexi hugged her rag doll, looking both cold and tired. "That's very kind of you. I just don't want to get you into any trouble." She thought of the man she'd seen looking from the window on the third floor. "Did you say there is no one else staying here?"

"Just the three of us," he said, smiling down at Lexi. "I'm the security guard. Name's Elmer. Elmer Thompson. I'll be here until six, when the manager arrives with the rest of the crew finishing up the place. I'll let him know you're here."

Jenna had forgotten about Fred until he meowed and tried to jump down. "I'm sorry about the cat. He's my daughter's and she couldn't bear to leave him in the car."

Elmer smiled. "I think we can accommodate the cat, as well. The dining room isn't open yet, but I can scare up some canned tuna and a box with some sand from the construction site. How would that be?"

"Wonderful." Jenna found herself starting to relax. "I'll pay you, of course."

"You can discuss that with the manager in the morning," he said.

She noticed the old black-and-white photographs behind the registration desk. "When were those taken?"

"Opening night, June 12, 1936. The new owners rebuilt the place to make it exactly like the original, right down to the most minute detail."

"Rebuilt it?" She felt a chill as she squinted at the photo taken of a ballroom filled with people, the men in tuxedos, the women in fancy gowns and elaborate, expensive jewelry. "What happened to it?"

"Burned down opening night."

She jerked back from the photograph. "How horrible. Was anyone hurt?"

"Fifty-seven souls lost."

She felt her chest tighten. "These photographs…if they were taken during opening night…"

He nodded in understanding. "You're wondering how the photos survived. A newspaper photographer took the photos then left to meet his deadline not realizing that the hotel was burning to the ground as he drove into town."

She glanced around unable to hide her shock. "Why would anyone want to build on this site, let alone make the hotel exactly as it was?"

Elmer shook his head. "I've never met the owners, but I heard they feel Fernhaven is too beautiful to lie in ashes. They don't build hotels like this anymore, true enough, but quite frankly, I think they did it because of the ghosts."

"Ghosts?"

He laughed. "Haunted hotels are the thing, they tell me. It's a marketing ploy. Some of the crew have said they've felt them." He scoffed at the idea. "Cold spots in the hallways, curtains moving when there is no breeze, that sort of thing. The gimmick must work. We're booked solid for the grand opening in three weeks."

"It sounds ghoulish to me," Jenna said, and couldn't contain her shiver.

"I'm sorry. You're both chilled. Let me get you into a room." He turned to the wall of wooden cubbyholes behind the counter. Each held a pair of old-fashioned room keys. "I suppose I should have you sign in, if you don't mind. Make it official."

Elmer flipped open a thick book that looked not only old but charred in one corner, as if it had been burned. "From the original hotel," he said, seeing her shock. He swung the book around and handed her a pen.

She took the pen, but drew back when she saw the date on the opposite page: June 12, 1936. Seventy years ago. And the list of guests who'd signed in that night. She couldn't help but wonder how many of those people had died here.

"Is there a working phone in the room, so I can call for a wrecker in the morning?" she asked.

"Yes."

She noticed that his attention was suddenly fixed on the key to room 318, lying next to the registration book. He seemed surprised to see it there. She tried to remember if she'd seen him take it from the cubbyhole, and couldn't.

Frowning, he checked the book, then with a shake of his head and a small laugh, he handed her the key with 318 embossed on it.

"Thank you." Jenna looked again at the old photographs of people dancing in a large ballroom, others sitting in the lobby or standing at a long bar.

One of the faces jumped out at her. Her heart began to pound for seemingly no reason as she stared at a man from the 1936 photograph.

He was lounging against the bar, decked out in a tux, holding a champagne glass in his hand as he smiled at the camera, arrogance in every line of his body.

His hair was dark, with an errant lock hanging down over his forehead. His features were as chiseled as the broad shoulders under the tux jacket, his face handsome even with the thin dark mustache.

She felt a chill ripple across her skin. Something about the man reminded her of the image she'd seen in the third-floor window earlier, as she and Lexi had approached the hotel.

The man seemed to be looking right at her—and smiling as if he knew something she didn't.

"If you'll just sign the book…"

She dragged her gaze away from the photograph, surprised she'd been so drawn to it she'd completely forgotten to sign in.

She started to write her full name, then stopped. For a few moments, with everything that had happened, she'd forgotten what she really had to fear. Not ghosts, but Lorenzo. She signed her name as Jenna Johnson and made up an address in Oregon. Best not to even use her maiden name, McDonald. Lorenzo would be after her. Might already be hot on her trail.

"I'll bring up the tuna and cat box. If you like I can scare up something for the two of you to eat," Elmer offered.

"That is very kind of you, but not necessary." She had some cereal and dried fruit in her purse for Lexi. "We'll be fine tonight." At least, she hoped so.

"Are your suitcases in your car?" he asked. "If you give me your keys, I'll run down and get anything out that you might need for tonight," he offered.

"Oh, that's not necessary. I feel like we have imposed on you enough."

"Please. I get bored to tears here. It's nice knowing there is someone else in this big old place. And you and your daughter are going to need dry clothing."

He was right, Jenna thought. "Thank you," she said, as she handed him the keys.

"The elevator to your wing is right down there," Elmer told her. "I'll be up in a few minutes with your things."

"Come on, Mommy." Lexi pulled on her hand.

"Thank you," Jenna said again to the security guard. She felt shaken and weak, stumbling around in a haze of exhaustion. A little rest and she'd be fine. Thank goodness the hotel had been here. She didn't know what she would have done otherwise.

Her daughter broke free again to skip toward the elevator, her eyes bright with excitement.

The lobby seemed too large and empty as Jenna followed. The elevator doors opened as if expecting them.

Jenna took Lexi's hand and stepped into the empty elevator car. But as the doors closed and the mirrored, wood-paneled cage began to hum upward, she had the strangest feeling that they weren't alone.

HARRY BALLANTINE STOOD in the corner of the elevator wondering what he was doing. What had he expected? That there was some reason he felt drawn to this woman? That maybe she'd been sent here?

She was totally oblivious of him. Just like the little girl and the cat.

He noticed the diamond ring on the woman's left hand. She was turning it nervously with her thumb. True to his former profession as a con man and jewel thief, he assessed the diamond in the half second it took to do so. Not bad quality. An average cut. A carat and a quarter. Not worth stealing.

The thought surprised him. He hadn't thought about stealing anything in years.

His gaze went to the woman again. Who was she? But more to the point, what was it about her that had him thinking about the past again?

He'd almost forgotten what it had been like, the night of Fernhaven's first grand opening. Standing at the bar watching the men in tuxedos, the women in expensive gowns, all whirling around the spacious ballroom to the music of the Johnny Franklin Orchestra.

Those had been the days. Harry had been thirty-two and had never seen that much wealth in one room before. Not surprisingly, he'd been down on his luck—until he'd conned his way into an invitation to the grand opening.

June 12, 1936.

It had been nothing short of heaven for a jewel thief.

Until the fire.

The elevator slowed. The woman glanced in his direction, and for just an instant he thought she might have sensed him there.

JENNA LEANED AGAINST the elevator wall, the past few days finally catching up with her as she stared at the empty space across from her, telling herself no one was staring back at her and Lexi.

Her reflection in the elevator mirrors made her wince. Not only did she look terrified, but there were dark circles under her eyes and her face was pale and drawn. Her hair hung limply from her ponytail.

The elevator ride seemed interminable but she was sure it only took a few seconds before the car stopped.

As the doors hummed open Lexi looked up, breaking into a smile as if there was someone waiting just outside the elevator. Jenna felt a cold draft curl around her neck. There was no one standing there. Nor did she see anyone in the long, lush red carpeted hallway.

"Did you see her hat?" Lexi asked. "It was purple."

Jenna had no idea what her daughter was talking about. She gripped Lexi's hand as the elevator seemed to fill with the icy invading air, and practically lunged out, dragging Lexi with her.

Before the doors closed behind them, Jenna turned to look back, expecting to see frost on the mirrors. The elevator was empty, her reflection mocking her fear.

"Come on," Jenna said in a whisper as she led Lexi down the hall.

Lexi took off, skipping along the plush carpet of the wood-paneled hallway.

"Wait!" Jenna called quietly, even though according to the security guard there were no other guests to disturb. The wing was deathly still.

She was so tired that just lifting each foot took Herculean effort. When she saw the room, she gasped in astonishment. Elmer had said it was a suite, but she hadn't expected this.

She looked at the magnificent rooms, half-afraid to enter. Lexi had already disappeared inside, making Jenna nervous. She stepped into the suite and closed and locked the door.

For just a moment she felt something—a cool brush against her cheek. She drew back, touching her skin.

She couldn't rid herself of the feeling that she and Lexi weren't alone, hadn't been since they'd entered Fernhaven. Jenna was afraid that somehow Lorenzo had followed her. She told herself that was crazy. Unless he had some sort of tracking device on the SUV…

Ridiculous. He had no reason to track himself. Unless one of his so-called "associates" had put the device on his car.

Jenna knew she was being paranoid. No way could Lorenzo have found them, let alone sneaked into the suite to wait for them.

Lexi came running out of a far bedroom, chattering to her rag doll as she climbed up to look out the bay windows. "Lookee, Mommy!" she cried in delight.

Jenna joined her to gaze down at a beautiful courtyard. Lights glowed golden on an exquisite fountain and a string of hot pools set among huge rocks with steam rising from them. Past the pools there appeared to be a path that disappeared into the foggy darkness and thick foliage of the mountainside.

It was all beautiful and eerie. Jenna hugged herself, trying to enjoy this extraordinary place as much as her daughter obviously was.

She told herself to be glad that she had Lexi back. That they were safe now. But the words were hollow. She knew Lorenzo. He wouldn't stop until he found her, until he destroyed her.

Lexi raced across the large suite to peer out another window. Jenna followed again and saw that this side looked down on the front of the hotel.

Beyond the small parking lot was the thick darkness of the forest. Jenna stared into the blackness, imagining someone staring back at her, then hurriedly pulled the drapes and turned toward the larger of the two bedrooms.

A knock at the door startled her. "Who is it?"

"Elmer Thompson."

She recognized the aging voice of the security guard from downstairs and felt foolish. Hadn't he told her that there was no one other than the three of them in the entire hotel tonight?

She opened the door and he rolled a cart in. She caught a glimpse of Lexi's and her suitcases.

Fred started meowing as Elmer handed her a can of tuna and an opener. She opened the can and fed the cat as Elmer took Lexi's small princess suitcase into the second bedroom, along with the box of sand.

"I took a look at your car," he said as he rolled the cart out of the master bedroom after unloading it. "I'm afraid the front axle is broken. It's definitely not drivable."

She would have to call for a rental car first thing in the morning and have the SUV towed to the nearest town.

"Sorry. You've had your share of bad luck tonight," he added. "But at least you're someplace warm and dry and safe." He smiled. "I'll be downstairs until six. Just call if you need anything else."

"You've been too kind," Jenna said, and tried to tip him.

"Thank you, but no. I'm just happy to help."

He left, and she got Lexi into some clean dry pj's and into bed.

By the time she entered the other bedroom, all she wanted to do was fall into bed still wearing her damp clothing.

But as she stepped into the room, she saw her suitcase on an ornate stand at the end of the bed. Beside it was a large navy blue duffel bag she'd never seen before.

She frowned, wondering where it had come from. It must have been in Lorenzo's car, but it didn't look familiar.

She stepped toward it, feeling a sense of panic as she slowly unzipped the bag and peeled back the top.

The duffel was filled with stacks of used hundred-dollar bills! There had to be thousands of dollars in the bag.

She stumbled back from it. *No. Oh no.* Her

body began to quake with the realization of what she'd done.

She hadn't just taken Lorenzo's daughter or his SUV. She'd taken his *money*.

Chapter Four

"Mommy, you didn't tuck me in, the way you always do," Lexi said behind her.

Jenna jumped, clamping a hand over her mouth to keep from crying out. She fought back the tears of fear and frustration that burned her eyes as she turned to face her daughter, and tried to smile.

"What's wrong, Mommy?" Lexi asked, her lower lip protruding as she studied her face.

"Nothing. You just startled me, that's all."

Lexi looked as if she might cry.

"Everything's fine, sweetie," Jenna said, leading her back to the other room.

It was so late all she wanted to do was go to bed, but she was determined to try to keep to their usual routine for Lexi's sake.

But she knew she had to get the money back to

Lorenzo somehow, and quickly. Maybe if she gave it back…

She shook her head at even the thought that it would appease her ex-husband. Nothing would placate him but revenge. Still, she had to try. For Lexi's sake.

The question was how to get it to him. She couldn't just box it up and send it by UPS.

Lexi scrambled up onto the bed and began to jump up and down. "Three little monkeys jumping on the bed—" She broke off in a fit of giggles. The words were from their favorite book.

"No jumping on the bed! I don't want you falling off and busting your head," Jenna said, playing along.

Lexi plopped down, still giggling. "I like it here. I want to live here."

No chance of that, even if Jenna had shared her daughter's enthusiasm for the place. They had to keep moving. As much as Jenna hated it, they would have to leave the country. Even with the safeguards she'd taken, she feared Lorenzo would find them, though, because in her heart she believed she would never be free of him.

Unless she was dead.

Or he was.

"I want to live here with you and Clarice and

Fred and—" Lexi's lower lip came out and tears filled her eyes "—a new daddy who's nice."

Jenna felt her heart break for her daughter. She'd stayed with Lorenzo as long as she had only because she'd wanted Lexi to have a father. She realized now that she'd been hoping that maybe Lexi's love could change her father. Jenna had been such a fool.

"You have sweet dreams, okay?"

Lexi nodded.

Jenna tucked her daughter into bed and kissed her warm forehead, brushing back a lock of her hair. Lexi had her coloring, the light skin, the dark brown eyes and hair, although Lexi's hair was darker than Jenna's, more like her father's, thick and straight.

Lexi had taken after Jenna in personality as well, and fortunately didn't have any of Lorenzo's traits, including his need for perfection or his bad disposition. Jenna was thankful for that.

"Good night. Sleep tight. Don't let the bedbugs bite," Jenna murmured, after Lexi had said her prayers.

The little girl laughed. "There aren't any bedbugs."

"No," Jenna agreed. Not in this hotel. She was feeling better about staying here. Even Fred had come out from under the bed.

The suite, she had to admit, *was* beautiful, from the rich woods to the soft carpet and elegant furnishings.

Lexi snuggled down in bed, with Clarice tucked on one side and Fred on the other.

Jenna padded to the door and looked back at her daughter. She could hear Lexi carrying on a one-sided, whispered conversation with the rag doll. Her daughter had such an active imagination. She could entertain herself for hours. Lorenzo used to say it wasn't normal. That they should have another child for Lexi to play with. He'd tricked Jenna the first time. But she'd been too smart for him after that.

Studying her daughter from the doorway, she was just thankful that Lexi hadn't seemed to suffer, not through the divorce or her abduction by either parent. Since she'd never known "normal," Lexi didn't seem to realize that her parents *had* divorced. Or that she and her mother were running for their lives.

To the comforting sound of Lexi's sweet voice, Jenna checked the entire suite to make sure there was no one hiding there. Relieved, and finally starting to relax, she went into her bedroom and opened her suitcase.

She hadn't packed much, just a few clothes for herself, and most of Lexi's. She'd had to move quickly once she'd gotten the call from the private investigator, telling her that he believed her ex-husband had taken Lexi back to the home Jenna had shared with him.

"Let the police handle getting your daughter back," the private investigator had advised.

"I've already tried that route." The man obviously didn't know Lorenzo Dante. "This is something I have to do myself."

Stripping off the black clothing now, she tossed it aside and put on the complimentary thick white, terry-cloth guest robe hanging in the closet. She pulled it around her, snuggling into the warmth, trying to chase away the chill that ran bone deep, as she looked at the duffel bag full of money.

Hurriedly, she zipped it closed and stuffed it into the back of the closet. Tomorrow she would figure out a way to get it to Lorenzo.

In the meantime, she and Lexi were safe, she thought, repeating it like a mantra. At least for tonight.

She couldn't wait to soak in the huge old-fashioned tub. Maybe tonight, for the first time in a long time, she would be able to sleep.

Or maybe not, she mused, as she sensed that same strange charge in the air that she had earlier. It breezed past her, a brush of icy breath against her bare skin, leaving her with that sense of a presence in the room with her.

She checked the whole suite once again, unable to stop herself. There was no one there, just as there hadn't been earlier.

Back in her bathroom, she began to fill the enormous tub with hot steamy water and almond-scented bubble bath, compliments of Fernhaven.

She shied away from thinking about Lorenzo. Or the money in the duffel bag in the back of her closet. To her surprise, her thoughts veered to the man in the old black-and-white photograph from the hotel's opening night. Funny how she thought she could smell the smoke from his cheroot....

With a shudder she realized that the man in the old photograph resembled the one she'd thought she'd seen at the window of the third-floor hotel room tonight.

But that wasn't possible. There was no one else in the hotel, Elmer had said.

Jenna frowned. Lexi was the one with the overactive imagination, not her.

Exhaustion, she decided. What else could it be?

A low hissing sound directly behind her made her whirl around. Fred was crouched in the doorway of the bathroom, his wide-eyed gaze boring into the corner of the window seat across from her.

Jenna stared at the spot where Fred's eyes were transfixed. There was no one there, of course.

She snatched up the cat.

"Fred, I really wish you wouldn't do that," she said as she carried him back to Lexi's room. He protested as she started to close the door so he couldn't get out. "I'm not going to have you waking me up all night with that foolishness," she whispered.

He just stared at her with those big eyes, then looked past her, jumping as if someone frightening had just come up behind her.

She swung around, knowing even as she did that no one would be there. Then she glared down at Fred, who had stopped hissing, but seemed to be watching the doorway, as if whoever had been there had left.

"Honestly, Fred, you're really starting to annoy me," she whispered, scratching his ears. He began to purr, pushing against her fingers, golden eyes closed in contentment. "Oh, how quickly you change your tune, you old faker."

She moved to the bed to reassure herself that Lexi was sleeping soundly. The child's face was angelic in sleep. She had Clarice tucked in the crook of her arm. Jenna leaned down, needing to touch her daughter, to assure herself that she was real, that she was here, that she was safe.

Jenna pressed a soft kiss on her baby girl's cheek, then remembered the water running in the tub in her bathroom. Closing the bedroom door, she rushed back and hurriedly turned off the faucet before the tub overflowed. Then, unable not to, she looked at the spot Fred had freaked over. Nothing but an empty, sparkling tile bench.

That's what she hated about cats. They jumped at nothing and generally spooked her. Darn that cat. She couldn't help herself, but now she was scared again. She rubbed the back of her neck, unable to throw off the memory of that cold draft, and Fred's odd behavior.

But it wasn't just the cold. Or the cat. It was the feeling of being watched.

She stared down at the tubful of steamy water and glistening bubbles, smelled the almond-scented bubble bath and yearned to sink into it.

"You aren't going to keep me from this bath," she said to the empty room, then directed a challenging glare at the tile bench.

Still, she disrobed hurriedly, stepping in and sliding down into the hot water until all but her head was under the bubbles. Her gaze went to the corner of the window seat again as she tried to assure herself that she was alone in the bathroom, that no one was sitting in the corner, watching her.

HARRY BALLANTINE SAT ON the tile bench, idly watching the woman through the steam.

The cat had sensed him. He wasn't sure what to make of that, any more than he was sure why he was here, in this room, with this woman.

The cat had spooked her. But she was no more aware of him than before, he thought with a disappointment he should have gotten over years ago.

She didn't know he was here. No one did.

Except maybe the cat. But who could tell with cats? They reacted to all kinds of things that weren't there.

Harry studied the woman.

He'd always been good at sizing up people. Had to be in his former line of work. He had been able to tell a lot by the way they dressed, their body language, their actions, the way they talked.

But his skills were rusty from lack of use.

She glanced toward him again, her big brown eyes dark and a little afraid.

What is your story?

Earlier, he'd watched her search the suite three times. Who did she think she was going to find here? Harry couldn't help but wonder what monsters she feared were hiding in the closet, waiting for her to turn out the light.

She was running from something. Someone. He'd bet everything he had on that. If he had anything to bet.

She was humming softly to herself now. Probably her version of whistling in the dark, since it was a child's song she was humming.

He'd seen the way she was with her daughter, love shining in her eyes whenever she looked at the child. He'd felt something like loss as he'd watched her. He couldn't remember his mother ever looking at him like that.

Not that she'd been mean to him. She hadn't. She'd just been too busy cooking, cleaning and taking care of nine kids, along with working in the fields with his father.

Jenna moved on to Broadway show tunes. He smiled, watching her hum away, her breath making the soap bubbles glide across the water's surface like tiny white sailboats.

He could see she was beginning to relax. Steam rose off the water, making her dark hair curl around her face. She brushed it back from her cheek.

She was pretty with her hair wet, her face bathed in steam. Her eyes were a different brown. He tried to think of the color as she blew out a breath and sent more bubbles scooting across the water.

He wondered what kind of trouble she'd gotten herself into. And why he felt so strongly drawn to her.

Harry slid off the seat and moved to the side of the tub. Steam rose from the hot water. She looked soft and lush in all that warmth, her head tilted back against the white porcelain, eyes closed, her dark hair wet and slick, falling like a waterfall down the side of the tub.

He couldn't help himself. She looked so young, so appealing, so vulnerable. Her skin was fair, dotted with a faint sprinkling of golden freckles across her cheekbones. He brushed his fingers over her warm, wet cheek, trailing them like falling stars. He'd forgotten what warm skin felt like.

Her whole body went rigid, her brown eyes widening.

He touched a finger to her full lips to see if they were as soft as they looked.

She jerked up into a sitting position, her breasts bobbing above the bubbles, full and round, the peaks dark and dripping wet.

She had felt his touch!

He quickly stepped back as she looked in his direction, even though he knew she couldn't see him.

Her pulse throbbed in her slim throat. Her eyes

were wide and dark, reminding him of a thunder-storm. She pressed a hand to her collarbone. He could see her listening like an animal, alert, prepared to fight. Or run.

She bit down on her lower lip. Her eyes filled with tears, and after a moment, her fingers came out of the bubbles to cover the spot where he had touched her lips. Tears threatened to spill over just before she ducked under the water and bubbles.

She had felt him! How was that possible?

He watched her dark hair float on the surface as he waited for her to come up for air.

Her head burst up out of the water and she gasped for breath, flipping her mane of wet hair back in a wave of warm scented water that splashed onto the floor.

Her eyes were closed, the lashes dark on her pale skin, as she wiped soap bubbles from her face.

In all these years, he'd never wanted to have substance and warmth—all the things that had once made him human—more than he did at that moment.

He stepped back, surprised not only by the strength of that long-suppressed emotion, but by something else that had been foreign in him: desire.

He watched her grope for the towel hanging on the rod within inches of her fingers. Without thinking, he pulled it down so it fell into her hands.

Her whole body went rigid again. Holding the towel out of the water, she sat up, wiped the soap from her face and opened her eyes to look anxiously around the room once more.

Keeping the towel in front of her, she stood up in the tub. He backed out of the room. He hadn't realized how much he'd missed the feel of a woman's skin. Jenna Dante's cheek had been soft and warm, just like her lips. God, how he'd missed warmth.

In her bedroom, the covers were turned down. A long black nightgown lay across the pillow. Silk. He heard her pull the plug in the tub. The water began to drain noisily. Even the bedroom smelled of almond from her bath. He inhaled the last of the scent as if it was water and he was a man dying of thirst.

He felt a strange intimacy with this woman. Why, after seventy years of a kind of hell?

Her purse was on the nightstand. He could hear her in the bathroom, brushing her teeth. He knew without looking that she had dried her body quickly and wrapped herself again in the guest robe.

In her purse he found the usual female stuff, along with two grand in traveler's checks. Her driver's license said her name was Jenna McDonald. Not Johnson, the name she'd registered under.

In a manila envelope in her purse he found copies of vaccinations and medical histories for herself and her daughter. Also in the purse were her birth certificate and one for her daughter, Alexandria, two plane tickets in the names Nancy and Alicia Clark, and two passports with the kid's and her photographs, in the new names. The woman had to have a connection to get these—a criminal element.

He glanced toward the bathroom as she finished brushing her teeth and shut off the water. She was running away all right. Far away, from the looks of it, and not planning to come back. From the husband?

A quick search of her suitcase turned up nothing of interest. He glanced in the closet and spotted a large, heavy-looking, navy blue duffel bag on the floor. Interest piqued, he took a look.

The duffel was filled with hundred dollar bills, used ones, banded together in what he would guess were ten or twenty thousand dollar stacks.

He'd never seen that much money in one bag

before, but he'd always wanted to. He felt that old pull like a bad ache. Once a thief, always a thief.

Her black clothing had been thrown over the chair near the bed. He picked up the jacket, wondering what was so heavy that it pulled down one pocketed corner.

A gun. The woman had a gun! He didn't need to pick it up to see that it was fully loaded.

For all he knew she was running from the cops. Or even the feds, given that wad of money in the closet.

What kind of trouble was this woman in?

She came out of the bathroom wrapped up tight in the bathrobe, just as he'd known she would be. Nor was he surprised when she checked the suite again. He watched her open her daughter's bedroom door.

He could see the relief in Jenna's body as she knelt over her child, tucking the little girl in with a tenderness that touched him.

All these years he had felt nothing. Why now? And for a woman who was in more trouble than Harry wanted to know about?

He hovered beside her bed, watching her fall asleep. Watching the rise and fall of her chest, the slight flutter of her eyelashes on her pale skin.

Her cheeks were still flushed from her bath.

She smelled heavenly. At least what he thought heavenly would smell like.

He'd never really noticed her mouth before. It was bow-shaped. There was a light sprinkling of freckles across her nose and a tiny brown spot, like a fleck of chocolate, just below her left ear.

He wanted to touch her. He felt drawn to her in ways he didn't understand. But something told him he'd been waiting a lifetime for her.

He joined her on the bed, lying next to her, listening to the steady rhythm of her breathing, content for the first time in seventy years.

Chapter Five

Lorenzo was disappointed when he woke to realize that Jenna was still alive, still had his daughter and his money. Killing her had only been a dream.

Unfortunately, his current situation *wasn't* a dream, but a nightmare. Franco was dead. Valencia's money was gone. And the clock was ticking. Lorenzo needed that money found one way or another. And soon.

He also needed to make sure that if Franco really *did* have a girlfriend she wouldn't be talking to Valencia.

Getting up, he pulled a red silk robe over his naked body and went to the top of the stairs, stopping to survey the living room. He'd cleaned up last night. There was no sign of anything out of place—just the way Lorenzo liked it. He couldn't have gone to bed without sweeping up the glass and scrubbing the blood off the tile.

While he'd taught Jenna to keep his house immaculate, the way he insisted, Alexandria had driven him crazy with her toys and dropping food on the floor at the table. He'd blamed Jenna for not making their daughter behave better.

He had to admit his life was easier without Jenna and Alexandria. But once he had his daughter to himself he would teach her not to make messes. Jenna had always been too easy on the child. Lorenzo saw now that he should have been stricter with both of them.

He went to the drawer where he'd put Franco's wallet and cell phone—and the plastic gloves he'd worn to remove them from Franco's body.

Donning the gloves again, he went through the wallet, finding only cash and one gas credit card, in Valencia's name. No photographs. Nothing personal.

Lorenzo pocketed the seventy-five dollars in cash, thinking what a two-bit thug Franco had been. Didn't even carry enough cash to buy a decent meal.

Booting up the cell phone, he checked Franco's phone directory. Only one number in it. Not surprisingly, it was Valencia's. He checked the list of calls Franco had received. All from Valencia. Sheesh, Franco had no life.

Or at least no life he wanted anyone to know about.

Lorenzo then checked numbers dialed. For a moment it looked as if all of those would be to Valencia, as well. All except one.

He dialed the number, not holding out much hope. A woman answered and tore right in. "Franco. I was worried about you. I waited up half the night for your call." She stopped. "Franco?"

Lorenzo hit End and put the wallet and cell phone into a plastic grocery bag. He pulled off the gloves and disposed of them in his garbage.

Getting the woman's address proved easy. The number Franco had called was to a land line. He found her through his computer's cross directory. Her name was Rose Garcia. She lived on Beacon Hill. While still on the Internet, he called up a map directory and printed out a route to the woman's house—and ordered a rental car.

Jenna had taken his only form of transportation. The memory did little to improve his mood. Worse, she'd left her car behind—but he no longer had a key for it.

The rental agency promised to bring him a car at once, something big and black.

He then called a towing service. The sooner he got rid of Jenna's car the better.

Under normal circumstances, he would have had a leisurely breakfast and taken a soak in his whirlpool bath before going out. But thanks to Jenna, nothing was as it should be. Since he couldn't put off getting to Rose Garcia before Valencia did, he'd be lucky to get something to eat before noon.

Jenna, now that she had the duffel bag of money, was probably eating a nice big room service breakfast in some fancy hotel.

The thought ruined his day.

JENNA WOKE TO RAIN. It plinked against the window, driven by a harsh wind.

She rose at once and went to check on Lexi. Her daughter was sleeping like an angel, and Jenna felt such relief it brought tears to her eyes.

She climbed into bed next to her and snuggled close, breathing in the sweet scent.

Lexi stirred, rolling over, her big brown eyes widening in surprise to find her mother in her bed.

"What are *you* doing here?" the little girl asked, smiling.

"I got cold and got in bed with you," Jenna said. It was one of the excuses that Lexi used when she didn't want to sleep alone.

Lexi smiled, recognizing it, and gave her an I-know-better look. "I had a dream about the ocean," she said, and proceeded to tell about swimming in the salty surf. "I had a big dog that ran in the water and splashed me. The dog was black and white and had floppy ears and a big tongue." Lexi giggled at the memory.

Jenna smiled at her daughter, thankful that the dream had been a pleasant one. Her own dreams had been disturbing. "That sounds like a wonderful dog. But what did Fred think about that?"

As if on cue, Fred crawled over them to let out a loud meow, making it clear he wanted his breakfast.

Jenna hated that they had to get up and get going. She would have loved to stay in the bed, talking and giggling with Lexi.

Or go back to sleep. Back to the dream. It felt unfinished. She flushed with heat at the memory of the man in it. The dream had left her frustrated and aching for fulfillment. For release. Worse, she'd dreamed about the man from the old photograph.

How odd was that? But she knew she'd probably conjured him up because he was safe. The photo had been taken seventy years ago. The man had been about her age then. He was long dead, long forgotten. Safe.

Jenna swung her legs over the side of the bed and stretched. Her body felt too alive, her skin tingling as the dream refused to fade.

"I put some clothes out for you to wear," she said over her shoulder to her daughter as she headed for her own bathroom. "And no bouncing on the bed!"

The bedsprings instantly quieted, making her smile.

As she walked through the living area, she noticed that the hotel suite seemed less ominous in daylight.

She went to the window and looked out at the rain-drenched mountainside. The courtyard itself was still shrouded in fog. She dreaded just the thought of driving off this mountain in such poor visibility. Or was it leaving the dream that she dreaded?

She called for a rental car—and wrecker—and was told both would be sent as soon as possible.

"I don't want to leave," Lexi moaned from the bed. "Clarice and Fred don't, either."

Jenna looked back at Lexi's pouty face.

It was so cute, she had to smile. "We'll play a game on the way into town. We can have breakfast at the first café we see." She thought of Lexi's dream of running on the beach with a dog. She didn't see why they couldn't have a dog someday. Or why they couldn't live on the beach. "How would you like to go to the ocean?"

Lexi's eyes lit up as she scrambled to her feet and began to bounce on the bed again. Fred dug his claws in to hang on, making them both laugh as Lexi bounded off the bed, then jumped back on to retrieve her doll.

"We're going to the ocean," Lexi told Clarice. "That's where we're going to live. We'll have a new daddy, a nice daddy, and a dog." She turned to Jenna. "What is the name of our dog?"

Jenna could only shake her head, her heart breaking all over again at Lexi's wish for a new daddy. "You'll have to pick a name for your dog. Now hurry and dress so we can get going."

Lexi did so, mumbling under her breath to her doll things Jenna was sure she didn't want to hear.

As she padded to her bedroom, the dream hung around her like a cocoon, images flitting in and out, vague and muddled. But that desperate feeling of wanting, of needing, made Jenna ache.

The harder she tried to remember the dream, the more it evaded her. But she could still almost feel him. His presence, his touch, his essence.

"Sexual frustration," she said with a grin. Her laugh sounded hollow even to her own ears.

The dream had felt so *real*. The warmth of him. Lying in his arms, his touch arousing her in ways—

She stopped, staring down at the bed, as her body turned to ice. Her heart began to pound erratically.

There were two impressions in the down-covered mattress. One on her side, where she always slept. The other where someone else had lain next to her.

Chapter Six

There was only one thing Raymond Valencia hated more than being treated like a fool, and that was allowing someone to *think* he was one.

Lorenzo Dante's story didn't hold water. Franco wouldn't cross him. At least not on his own.

Raymond could think of only two ways in which Franco could be coerced into doing something so stupid as stealing from the man who'd picked him up out of the gutter.

One would be if he had no other choice. Like a knife to his privates. But even that was hard to believe, given that Franco knew Raymond would do far worse to him when he caught him.

Two would be by a woman. If Lorenzo was right, some female had Franco confused. Raymond knew that a woman could turn any man's head around. But Franco? Franco had women, of course. But he made no secret that they were only the kind he paid for, the kind a man could depend on not to let him down.

Was it possible Franco had an honest-to-goodness girlfriend he hadn't let on about?

"You know anything about Franco having a girlfriend?" he asked one of the two men he'd called the moment Franco hadn't shown up.

Both men, now weary from lack of sleep, shook their heads. "I never saw him with anyone," Rico said. Rico was small, wiry and deadly. Raymond never turned his back on the man.

"You never heard him talking on his cell to any broad?" he asked the other man, a massive Neanderthal everyone called Jolly, short for Jolly Green Giant. Jolly was anything but.

"I never heard nothin'," Jolly said.

Raymond studied the expressions of the two men: bored and half-asleep, but seemingly not hiding anything. "Okay, Jolly, I want you to find the girlfriend."

"There *is* a girlfriend?" he asked in surprise.

"That's what you're going to find out," Raymond snapped. "Rico, I want you to take over the tail I have on Lorenzo Dante. If he blinks I want to know about it. Got it?"

Rico showed only slight surprise. There had never been any love lost between Rico and Lorenzo. Probably because they were so much alike. Another reason Raymond didn't trust Rico. Both were capable of killing their mothers without the least bit of remorse if there was something in it for them.

Raymond couldn't understand that. He'd bought his mother a huge house, sent her on expensive cruises, made sure she had everything she'd ever dreamed of. A man had to have someone in his life who loved him no matter what he did. That, Raymond had realized a long time ago, was only one person: his mother.

Lorenzo hadn't understood that. He hated his mother and instead had attempted to find love through marriage. Raymond had tried to warn him, but the man hadn't listened. Not that Raymond hadn't liked Jenna. In truth, he thought of his associate's wife with a deep-seated envy. Jenna had been too good for Lorenzo. The man hadn't known how to treat a woman like her and Lorenzo had lost her—and his child.

Lorenzo was a fool. He had proved he wasn't reliable. Raymond had been relieved when Lorenzo had offered to buy his way out of the business and leave the country.

But Jenna…well, she was another story. Raymond still didn't regret that he'd helped her during the divorce. Otherwise Lorenzo would have ended up with his daughter. A man like that had no business with a child like Alexandria. Raymond knew he'd done the right thing helping Jenna get her divorce. And with fake passports, he had trusted that she would never tell Lorenzo who had helped her.

But Raymond wondered now if Lorenzo had somehow found out the truth. The thought brought a cold dread. It would make Lorenzo a liability that had to be taken care of immediately.

The problem was that Lorenzo had friends. It wouldn't be good for business to hit Lorenzo. Especially now that Raymond was legit. It would be better if Lorenzo just left the country as he'd planned.

But if Franco hadn't taken his money and run off, then who did that leave? Lorenzo. And if Lorenzo had taken it, then he obviously was waging war.

Raymond checked to make sure the security system was on and the guard dogs were patrolling the area inside the fence around his house, just in case. So he'd have to find out who had taken his money—and why. First he would try to find

Franco and this alleged girlfriend. If that lead proved false, then he would have to deal with Lorenzo. If Dante had his money, Raymond would be justified in killing him. And killing him in the most painful way possible.

He started to pick up the phone to call Jenna. He felt a small thrill at just the thought of hearing her voice. But he was also worried. Lorenzo was a hothead. If he had found out that Raymond had helped Jenna, then the woman was in danger.

What would it hurt to call her and make sure everything was all right?

JENNA QUICKLY PACKED UP what little she'd unpacked last night, pulling the duffel out of the closet and putting it beside her suitcase. She couldn't stop shaking.

As she turned to put the last item in the suitcase she felt something brush by her. She caught her breath, freezing in place as the cool air caressed her cheek and trailed down her throat to the crest of her breasts above the silk gown. She leaned back, closing her eyes, caught again in the dream. She surrendered to it, washed with a yearning that made her tremble. And then it was gone.

She opened her eyes and looked around the empty room. My God, she was losing her mind.

These feelings, this fantasy… Upset with herself, she finished packing and angrily snapped shut the suitcase. What was wrong with her?

It was the hotel. The old photograph of the man at the bar. What had she seen in him that made her call him up in her dreams? She hated to think. He wasn't anything like Lorenzo, she realized. He was dark like Lorenzo and there was no doubt he had a confident air about him that verged on arrogance, but he was nothing like her ex.

How did she know that?

She felt a shiver. She couldn't know anything about the man in the photograph. But there had been a man who resembled him. The man she'd seen from the third-floor window when they'd arrived. Except according to the security guard, she and Lexi were the only guests here.

She'd imagined him. Because she needed someone to love?

Jenna scoffed at the idea. She wasn't sure she would ever trust another man. And the dream had nothing to do with love, but a whole lot to do with lust. She could well understand why she would imagine a gentle lover in her dreams. Even why she would draw him from out of the past to come to her. She'd never known a man's loving touch.

Lorenzo had been a fierce, brutal lover who took rather than gave.

Better to have a dream lover.

Except, Jenna thought with a frown, last night he'd only frustrated her. Made her want him, ache for him. She shivered, caught between desire and revolt. She didn't want to need any man—even a dream lover, but part of her feared he would return in her dreams tonight. Another part feared he wouldn't. She had the oddest feeling that he only existed for her here, in this eerie hotel with its ghosts.

How pitiful that if she wanted a man to love her with any tenderness, she'd had to find him in a dream.

She looked down at her left hand, to her engagement and wedding rings. She'd put them both back on, thinking it would make it easier to pretend to be married when she and Lexi were living in another country.

But just the thought of Lorenzo… She painfully wrenched both rings from her finger and threw them into her purse.

Jenna glanced back at the bed that she'd hurriedly made, leaving no sign of the impressions she'd thought she'd seen earlier. Imagined? Just as she'd imagined the man from the photograph coming to her in her dream?

Suddenly she just wanted out of this place. It made her feel things, sense things, yearn for things she couldn't have.

This hotel scared her. It was as if it knew her needs and desires. She and Lexi would be safer on the road than here, Jenna told herself. She was sure of it.

ROSE GARCIA GOT UP every morning and ran five miles no matter the weather. This morning it was drizzling. That's what she got for living in Seattle.

At the time she'd moved here, rain had seemed enjoyable compared to the winters where she'd grown up, in North Dakota. Her family had been Spanish royalty at some point, but her great-grandfather had gotten into trouble in Spain, been forced to catch a boat and light out for a new life. On the boat, he'd befriended some Norwegians and ended up a general store owner in North Dakota.

Rose stretched on the porch, listening to the drizzle turn to full-fledged rain as she prepared for her run. She loved living in Beacon Hill and had bought the house cheap because of the depressed area. But with the cost of houses around Seattle now, Beacon Hill was making a comeback. People like her were buying up the older houses and renovating them.

She'd done the work herself, watching those home improvement shows for tips. The guys she worked with made fun of her, but she could swing a hammer better than most and she was hell on wheels with a power saw.

She stretched her other leg, then quit stalling and bounded down the porch steps. As her luck would have it, the rain began to fall even harder. She ducked her head, burrowing down in her jacket, determined to do five miles even if it killed her.

It almost did.

A car came around the corner, moving too fast, as she was crossing the street. She lunged out of the way, feeling the bumper just miss her. The car's tire dropped into one of the potholes in the road. A wave of muddy water splashed over her, making her feel like a drowned rat.

She swore at the retreating car, noticing that it was black and expensive. The downside of an improving neighborhood, jerks like that one, she thought, and resumed her run, not worrying anymore about getting soaked by the rain.

LORENZO DANTE GLANCED back in his rearview mirror at the runner he'd almost hit, and cursed her. Stupid health nuts. Why didn't they join a gym like normal people? Or better yet, buy equipment and stay home?

Not that he wasn't already in a bad mood. And then to have some stupid pedestrian almost dent his rental car… He swore and slammed his fist on the steering wheel. Damn Jenna to hell and back. This was all her fault.

He was so angry he missed Rose Garcia's house address the first time and had to turn around and come back, circling the block, driving down the alley.

It was a small house. There were potted plants on the porch, checked curtains at the kitchen window, a red-and-white Mini Cooper out back. A house that said a woman lives here—*alone.*

But still he drove around the block a couple more times before he parked down the street. This didn't feel right. Franco and the woman who lived in that neat little house? Didn't add up.

Finally, taking his umbrella, he walked through the pouring rain up the steps to her porch and knocked softly, thinking she might still be in bed, since the car was out back.

No answer. He knocked a little harder, then surreptitiously peeked into her mailbox by the door. No mail. Glancing in a window, he saw that the place was neat, freshly painted, nice hardwood floors, modest carpets but well tended.

This was definitely not the kind of woman who would have dated Franco. Lorenzo wondered if he was dead wrong about her. But how could he be, after what she'd said when he'd called her number? She'd been expecting Franco to call her. She'd been worried about him. Had stayed up half the night. Sounded like a girlfriend. One who had Franco on a short chain.

Lorenzo double-checked the address, but remembered that she'd also sounded about the right age. Late twenties, early thirties.

He tried the number on Franco's cell phone for her. The phone rang and rang inside the house. No answer. She wasn't home. Someone must have picked her up.

He walked around back, and almost started to break into the rear door, but something stopped him. What if she had an alarm system? He decided a window was safer and, using his elbow, knocked out a pane.

No audible alarm went off as he reached through and unlatched the window. He shoved it up and, cleaning off the jagged glass, stepped through, annoyed his life had come to this.

Dusting off his favorite slacks, he ventured

deeper into the house just to make sure she wasn't home. Apparently she didn't have an alarm system. Stupid, trusting woman.

There weren't any photographs of Franco. No sign Franco had ever been in the house. Lorenzo was going through a desk drawer when the phone rang, making him jump.

He checked caller ID and recognized the number. One of Valencia's other thugs, Jolly. So Valencia had put him on the task of finding Franco's girlfriend. Lorenzo wondered how Valencia had latched on to Rose Garcia's number so fast without Franco's cell phone. Valencia must have supplied Franco with the phone.

Lorenzo couldn't help feeling relieved he'd gotten here when he had. Now if the chick would just get her butt home...

He'd barely had the thought when he heard footfalls on the porch. He flattened himself against the hall wall and waited as he heard the sound of a key in the lock. A gust of cool damp air brushed past him as he heard her open, close and lock the door.

If he'd guessed right, she would come walking by him at any moment. He waited. And waited. Then, straining, he heard what seemed to be her taking off her shoes at the door and cursing softly. He didn't have all day.

He peeked around the corner to see her stripping out of her wet clothing, and was shocked to realize that she was the runner he'd almost clipped with his car.

If only he'd known, he could have saved himself a lot of time and trouble. But then again, it would be better if she just disappeared. That would make it more believable that she'd talked Franco into taking off with the duffel bag of money.

She'd stripped down to a gray jogging bra and a pair of hot-pink bikini panties by the next time he stole another peek around the corner.

She wasn't what he'd expected, but he could definitely see why Franco had been interested in her. She was hot, late twenties–early thirties, in great shape.

She looked up as if sensing his presence. He jerked back, but realized he couldn't wait for her to come to him. Not now. Pulling his gun from behind him, he stepped around the corner of the wall.

"Hello," he said, pointing the barrel at her heart. "I'm a friend of Franco's. Scream and I'll kill you. Keep quiet and you get to live. Put your clothes back on. You and I are going for a little drive."

To his surprise, she didn't scream. She didn't

move. She glanced at the gun, then at his face. "I'm not putting those wet clothes back on."

Why couldn't he for once find a woman who just did what she was told? No, he always had to find one that put up an argument.

It was his last cognizant thought before she took a tentative step, seemed to wobble as if tired from her run, and flew at him. He never saw her foot coming until it slammed into the side of his head. He dimly felt her painfully twist the gun from his hand an instant before her other foot caught him in the groin.

But by then he couldn't isolate the pain, and he was already headed for the floor and unconsciousness, anyway.

ROSE BALANCED ON the balls of her feet, hopping back, poised to kick him again if necessary. She had the barrel of the gun trained on a kill spot just in case he was still conscious and lunged for her.

She waited a few seconds, then nudged him hard with her bare foot. Out cold.

She released the breath she'd been holding.

Lorenzo Dante. She'd recognized him right off. Until recently, he had been Raymond Valencia's top lieutenant. She'd heard he was planning to skip the country, and thought he'd already gone.

She wondered what he was still doing here. More to the point, what he was doing flat on his back in her living room.

Her mind worked up several scenarios before going with the one that seemed most likely. Only one person could have led him to her: Franco. And if that was the case, then Franco was dead.

She felt sick to her stomach as she stared down at the man on the floor. She'd known what she was getting into, but that didn't make it any easier now.

Whatever she did, she had to move fast. Had Valencia sent Lorenzo to take care of her, as well?

The phone rang, startling her. She edged around Lorenzo, just in case he decided to come to. She checked the caller ID and didn't recognize the number. A bad sign. The caller didn't leave a message. Another bad sign.

In the kitchen, she pulled a roll of duct tape from a drawer, noticing the window Lorenzo Dante had broken to gain entrance. Bastard.

It seemed a pretty good bet that if he didn't report in, someone would come looking for him. If they hadn't already. Best to make sure that Lorenzo didn't come to before she could decide what to do with him.

Back in the living room, she taped his wrists, ankles and mouth, then dragged him back into the kitchen, out of sight of the front door. She was chilled and trembling, her undergarments still soaked.

The hell with it, she thought as she ran upstairs, turned on the shower and stripped off the rest of her wet clothing before stepping in.

She would have loved to have stood under the hot spray long enough to really warm up, but that was too risky.

She shut off the shower and dried herself, listening for any sound that someone else had broken in. At least the next intruder would have easy entrance, thanks to Lorenzo Dante.

She dressed in jeans, a flannel shirt and boots, then took the packed small suitcase she kept for just such an occurrence. Back downstairs, she was relieved to see that no one else had shown up yet.

Lorenzo had come to, though. He was giving her the evil eye. She chuckled to herself, remembering her Spanish grandmother's evil eye. Lorenzo Dante, killer that he was, had nothing on Rose's grandmother, Rosamaria.

If he had found her, then she had to assume that Valencia knew, as well. She glanced around the house, bummed that she would have to leave her home. Even temporarily. As she headed for the back door, she heard Lorenzo trying to say something through the tape on his mouth.

Rose stopped. She knew she didn't have much time, but she couldn't help herself. She turned and went back, taking a perverse satisfaction when Lorenzo Dante, local tough guy, cried out in pain as she ripped the tape from his mouth.

"You bitch!" he screamed.

"I thought you had something important to say." She put down her bag and started to rip another strip of duct tape to reseal his mouth.

"No. Listen, I don't know who you are but maybe I can help you," he said quickly. "Franco's boss, Valencia, knows about you and Franco. He'll kill you if he finds you here."

She raised a brow. "Like you weren't going to."

He took a breath, obviously in some pain from at least one of the spots where she'd kicked him. That's what he got for breaking into her house and holding a gun on her.

"I will give you money so you can get away from him."

"Why would you do that?" she asked suspiciously. She heard a car go by slowly, for the second time in the past few minutes.

"Look, do you want the money or not?"

"Not." She started to slap tape back on his mouth.

"Wait! I don't think you realize who I am."

"Lorenzo Dante, two-bit criminal."

He winced at the two-bit part, just as she knew he would. "All you women are bitches. You're both going to burn in hell."

She had started to tape his mouth again but stopped. "What are you talking about?"

He closed his mouth and gave her a look that said over his dead body would he tell. Fine with her. She gave him a hard jab with the blade of her hand along his temple, then another just in case he didn't get the message.

"You and my ex-wife," he cried out, grimacing in pain. "I'll see you both in hell."

That she could believe. She slapped the tape over his mouth as she heard a car door slam out front.

She half expected one of Valencia's men to be covering the rear. The doorbell rang as she slipped out the back door to her car. Getting into her Mini, she turned the car key. The engine purred. She tromped on the gas, speeding out into the alley.

She spotted one of Valencia's men, Rico Santos, running along the side of the house with a gun in his hand. She reached the end of the alley, hung a quick right and didn't look back as she tried not to think of Franco and what the bastards had done to him.

She kept her foot pressed to the gas pedal, roaring down street after street, zigzagging her way toward Seattle, the skyline a dull gray in the pouring rain. When she was sure no one was following her, she slowed, pulled out her cell phone and called work.

"When was the last time anyone's seen Jenna Dante?" she demanded the moment she got her partner at the Seattle Police Department. She was afraid she already knew the answer.

"The chief called off the officer we had watching her after reading your report," Detective Luke Henry said.

Rose swore. "Does he realize that he probably signed Jenna Dante's death warrant?"

"She did that when she married Lorenzo and then decided to divorce him," Luke said solemnly.

True or not, Rose felt responsible. She was the one who'd gotten close to Jenna Dante, close enough that she'd been able to report that Jenna didn't know enough about her husband's business to turn state's evidence against him.

"My cover's blown," she said, feeling sick. "I think they made Franco."

Luke let out a pained sound. "How do you know that?"

"He called me on his way to Lorenzo's. He

said Lorenzo had sounded strange, almost angry. I think Franco was worried Lorenzo had somehow figured out who he was."

"Not possible. Not after spending two years undercover," Luke said. "Franco was in. Raymond Valencia trusted him like a son."

"Well, something went wrong." she said. "I got a call from Franco's cell and the caller hung up. Not long after that Lorenzo was holding a gun on me."

Rose swung the Mini toward the apartment complex where Jenna Dante had been living with her daughter.

"I just left Lorenzo trussed up like a Christmas turkey in my living room," she said. "One of Raymond Valencia's men had just arrived when I left. Rico Santos. You might want to send a squad car by so they don't tear up my house any more than they already have."

"Where can I reach you?" Luke asked.

"I'm going to try to find Jenna Dante." She hung up before he could remind her that she was on medical leave.

"TRAPPED?" Jenna echoed in disbelief. "For how long?"

Elmer shrugged. "Until they can get the road

open again none of us are going anywhere. The rental company you contacted this morning just called back. They can't get a car to you. The crew working on the hotel couldn't even get through. A bridge washed out to the west of us and the road is still flooded to the east."

"Surely there must be some other way out of here."

He shook his head. "Not until they get a road open, but don't worry. There is food stocked in the kitchen and so far the power hasn't gone out." He smiled. "It could be worse."

Yes, she thought, it definitely could be. If she couldn't get out of here, then Lorenzo couldn't get to her.

Still, she couldn't shake the feeling that she wasn't supposed to leave here, that her ending up here wasn't an accident.

That was crazy.

No crazier than the dream she'd had last night. She could still feel the effects of it. Crazy or not, a part of her didn't want to leave. She wanted *him* to come to her again.

Elmer was saying, "You might as well take advantage of what the hotel has to offer. At one time Fernhaven was famous for its healing waters. Have you seen the pools out back? They're sheltered from the weather and the water is nice and warm. As for breakfast, just help yourself in the kitchen."

Lexi started jumping up and down, wanting to go swimming.

"I guess we're going swimming," Jenna said, hoping to make the best of it for her sake. "We can raid the kitchen later."

"I'm going to be checking the rest of the hotel to make sure there aren't any problems," Elmer said. "Make yourselves at home." He seemed glad he wasn't trapped here alone.

She stood at the door to the suite and watched him disappear down the hall. The hotel had seemed isolated before, but nothing like now. It was just the three of them and a cat and a rag doll. Part of Jenna wanted to curl up in the room and wait out the storm—and the opening of the road.

But one look at her daughter's face told her that wasn't possible. "Let's get your swimming suit on."

Jenna got them both ready to go to the pools. It felt strange as they rode down the empty elevator.

Lexi rushed off, excited. She didn't seem to notice the brush of cold air as they exited the elevator.

"Wait a minute," Jenna told her. "There's something I need to do first." She didn't see Elmer at the registration desk. He must still be doing his check of the hotel.

She stepped behind the desk to take a closer look at the old black-and-white photograph of the men at the bar—one man in particular.

A chill rattled through her. That *was* the man who'd come to her in her sleep last night. She hadn't noticed before, but there were names written under some of the photographs. Under his, in small print, was the name Bobby John Chamberlain. The name had a line through it and under that name was another in a different handwriting: Harry Ballantine.

"Mommy," Lexi whined. "Come on."

Jenna swallowed hard as she stared into the man's eyes, then turned as Lexi began to run in circles crying, "Swimming, swimming, swimming."

Hurriedly Jenna spun the large, partially charred registration book around and did a quick scan for the name Harry Ballantine among the guests registered in 1936.

No luck. She quickly made a search for Bobby John Chamberlain. There it was. Room 318. The same room she and Lexi were staying in.

Why had the name been scratched out and Harry Ballantine written in? She shuddered, trying to tell herself it was a coincidence that she'd ended up in the same room. Vaguely, she remembered Elmer seeming flustered last night, as if he didn't recall choosing to put her in 318.

"Swimming!" Lexi cried.

"We're going swimming," Jenna said, her voice breaking as she took her daughter's hand and headed toward the pools.

Her hands were shaking, and as hard as she tried, she couldn't convince herself that it was just a coincidence she'd thought she'd seen the same man watching them from a third-floor room last night. That she'd dreamed about him. That she and Lexi were trapped here.

It was as if forces far beyond her control had not only brought her here, but were trying to keep her here.

Chapter Seven

Lorenzo jerked around on the floor, but as hard as he tried, he couldn't free himself. He'd never been so outraged in his entire life. And that was saying a lot. What made it unbearable was that Rico Santos, of all people, had to be the one to find him. He hated that son of a bitch.

"What you doin'?" Rico asked, standing over him, laughing.

Lorenzo mumbled a string of swearwords behind the thick tape on his mouth.

Rico laughed harder. "Sorry, I didn't catch that."

Lorenzo glared at him. If only looks really could kill.

And just when he thought things couldn't get any worse, Jolly showed up. Jolly and Rico had a good laugh, did some crude speculating on how

Lorenzo had ended up on the floor, gagged and bound, in some woman's house.

Lorenzo fought to free himself. If he could get loose he would kill them both and deal with the ramifications later.

"Oh, hold still, man," Rico said as he reached down and ripped the tape from his mouth.

It hurt like hell, but Lorenzo would have died before he showed it. He licked his lips. "Cut me loose."

"Take it easy," Rico warned, beady dark eyes narrowing as a switchblade appeared in his hand, the long slim shaft catching the light. "You see…" Rico leaned in so close that Lorenzo could smell what he'd had for breakfast "…Mr. Valencia wants us to bring you to him. He'd be upset if we had any trouble with you."

Lorenzo took a breath and let it out slowly. He would kill Rico. If not today, tomorrow. "Just cut the damn tape," he said quietly. "My legs are starting to cramp up."

Rico spun the switchblade in his fingers for a moment, then with a sudden thrust, sliced between Lorenzo's ankles.

Finally able to straighten his legs, Lorenzo rolled over onto his side and thrust out his wrists.

Rico met his gaze, holding it, while he freed his hands.

Lorenzo rubbed his wrists, staying prone on the floor until Rico finally rose and put the switchblade away.

Jolly offered Lorenzo a hand up. Jolly he would kill quickly. Rico was another story.

"Mr. Valencia is waiting." Rico's look said he knew Lorenzo would be coming for him, and he would be eagerly waiting.

Lorenzo couldn't believe how his luck had gone south. A woman had just kicked his butt. Worse, she'd gotten away. But maybe he could make that work to his advantage. If he couldn't find Rose Garcia, then neither could Valencia.

And who said she hadn't gone to meet up with Franco? Nobody.

His cell phone rang. He checked it. Alfredo. "Tell Valencia I'm on my way," he said to Rico and Jolly. "I need to take this."

Neither moved.

"He wants us to bring you to him," Jolly said. "Now."

Lorenzo swore silently. He didn't want to take the call in front of these two bozos, but he also could use a little good news right now. And if Alfredo had found Jenna, then that would be good news indeed.

"Yeah?" he said, after flipping open his cell phone.

"Just checking in like you said." Alfredo spoke in a low monotone no matter what was going on. "Found a gas station northeast of Seattle where she filled up. Clerk remembers her. She didn't ask for directions or nothing like that, so you want me to keep looking? A lot of wild country out here."

Lorenzo tried to hide his disappointment. "No, don't bother. Just come on back and I'll call you later." He snapped the cell phone shut and looked at the two men standing in front of him, telling himself he could take them both before either of them knew what hit 'em.

But killing two more of Valencia's men didn't seem the best idea right now.

"So what are we waiting for? Let's go see your boss. I'll follow you in my car."

"I think not," Rico said. "Jolly will bring you back for your car after you see the boss."

Just the thought of seeing Valencia on an empty stomach made him weak. "Mind if we stop and get breakfast along the way first? I'm starved."

Rico chuckled. "Yeah, right."

"We could swing through a drive-up," Jolly suggested. "I could use a little something."

"Fast food? Forget it," Lorenzo said, wondering again what his ex-wife was having for breakfast and where. "I'd rather starve."

ROSE GARCIA FLASHED her badge at Jenna Dante's apartment house and got the manager to open up 4B.

The apartment complex was a dump on the wrong side of town. After being married to a man with as much money as Lorenzo, Jenna had definitely taken a financial nosedive.

The manager was a short, squat, middle-aged bald man who smelled of fried onions. His name, according to the piece of paper taped to the door, was Buzz Gerard.

"I got things to do," Buzz said, scratching himself after he opened the door to Jenna Dante's apartment.

"So go do them." Rose stooped down to pick up the newspaper lying in the hall. She checked the date. This morning's. "I'll lock up when I leave," she assured him as she stepped into the apartment and closed the door behind her.

The place was neat and clean, nothing like the apartment complex itself. No sign of a struggle, she thought with relief. Or a break-in.

But it also had an empty, I'm-not-coming-back feeling, just as Rose had feared. The kitchen was clean, holding only a few odds and ends, dishes and silverware, thrift shop stuff.

Rose opened the closet. Empty hangers, some looking as if clothes had been jerked off in a hurry. She checked the daughter's room. Bed made. Room too neat. The bureau empty just like the closet.

Jenna had cleared out. With the girl? It appeared so. But where had she gone? And why?

Something must have spooked her.

Lorenzo, Rose thought. He'd sure as hell scared *her.*

Rose picked up the phone and checked caller ID. Jenna hadn't received many calls. The most recent one was from Flannigan Investigations. *Interesting.* Rose jotted down the other numbers, then checked the numbers Jenna had called. One stopped her cold.

Raymond Valencia? Why would Jenna call Lorenzo's boss?

Rose searched the rest of the apartment but didn't find anything to indicate where Jenna had gone. Clearly, however, she wasn't coming back.

Every instinct told Rose that Jenna Dante was in over her head. Maybe in more trouble than Jenna knew, if she was involved with Raymond Valencia.

RAYMOND VALENCIA WAS IN his greenhouse when he heard Jolly and Rico return. Rico had called to say they were bringing Lorenzo Dante with them.

Picking several of the finer tomatoes for lunch, Raymond left the greenhouse, the one place he found any kind of peace.

In the kitchen he gave the tomatoes to the cook, then found Jolly and Rico waiting in the den. Lorenzo had made himself at home in one of the leather chairs by the fireplace. He was slumped down a little, an ankle resting on his knee, his hand fiddling with the tassel on his Italian loafers as if he was bored. Or nervous.

He stopped fiddling the moment Raymond walked into the room. Nervous, Raymond decided. Very nervous. What had Lorenzo done? Raymond hated to think. He motioned for Jolly and Rico to leave them alone.

As the door closed behind them, Raymond took a chair facing Lorenzo. Crossing his legs, leaning back, hands in his lap, he imitated the other man's comfortable composure. Only Raymond really was relaxed.

"Don't you think it's time you told me what's really going on, Lorenzo?" he asked quietly.

Lorenzo pretended not to understand.

"What were you doing at Rose Garcia's house?"

"Just trying to help find Franco for you."

Raymond nodded. "When I talked to you last

night you said you didn't know Franco's girl-friend's name."

"This morning I realized that Franco had left his cell phone on my bar."

Raymond lifted a brow. "I thought Franco refused a drink last night."

"He did." Lorenzo had begun to sweat. "But I was behind the bar, so he came over to lean against it."

"Did he use the phone while he was there?"

Lorenzo seemed to consider that. "Not that I know of. But I had to leave the room to get the money. He could have called someone." He shrugged.

"Do you still have the phone?"

Lorenzo reached into his pocket, pulled it out and got up to hand the cell phone to him.

"You checked numbers dialed, right? That's how you found Rose Garcia?"

Lorenzo nodded. "I called the number this morning to make sure she was home."

"Why didn't you call me and tell me about this?"

"I thought I would find her, maybe get your money back and save you the effort."

Raymond smiled. "That was thoughtful of you." It was the weakest defense he'd ever heard.

As if Lorenzo Dante cared about anyone but himself. So how would finding Franco's girlfriend benefit Lorenzo?

"I understand this woman, Rose Garcia, got away?" Raymond asked.

Lorenzo nodded, looking sheepish. This, at least, appeared to be genuine. "She knew karate or some defense thing."

"Where is your ex-wife?"

Lorenzo's head jerked in obvious surprise. Raymond glimpsed panic in his eyes. "Why... what...why would you ask about Jenna?"

"Is there any reason she would leave town?"

Lorenzo blinked. "What makes you think she left town?"

Raymond said nothing.

Lorenzo's eyes widened. He shifted in his chair. "You think she ran off with Franco?" He looked dazed by the idea. "Jenna and Franco? You think they're together?"

The thought had never crossed Raymond's mind. "I thought you found Franco's girlfriend, this Rose Garcia woman."

"I guess I was wrong," Lorenzo said. "Jenna and Franco. Who would have known?"

Raymond tried to picture Jenna with Franco. Impossible. And yet Franco was gone with a bagful of money, and Jenna wasn't answering her cell phone.

And yet what bothered him wasn't how quickly Lorenzo had latched on to the idea but how he was taking it. Too calmly.

"That son of a bitch," Lorenzo spat, as if it had just sunk in. Or he'd just realized his reaction wasn't the right one. "I'm going to kill that bastard when I catch him."

"Not until I get my money," Raymond said, watching Lorenzo. This was all messed up. He couldn't have been that wrong about Jenna. Franco wasn't her type. But there *had* been a lot of money in that duffel. If Jenna had run off with Franco and the money, then it was out of desperation to get away from her ex-husband. Somehow this always seemed to come back to Lorenzo.

"I'll take care of it," Raymond told him. "I don't want you involved."

"But it's my ex—"

"Yes, it's your ex, exactly," Raymond said, cutting him off. "That's why I don't want you involved." He settled his gaze on Lorenzo. "You'd better hope this doesn't have anything to do with you."

"What?"

"If you're behind what is going on—"

"What? I'm responsible for Franco as well as a woman who divorced me?" Lorenzo looked angry as well as offended. "I let her divorce me just like you told me to. I even let her take my kid. How could I have been nicer to her?"

Chapter Eight

Flannigan Investigations was in Ballard, just north of downtown Seattle.

Rose couldn't help but wonder why Mike Flannigan's call had been the last one Jenna Dante received.

Recalling that private investigator Mike Flannigan had once told her he usually ate at his desk, she'd waited until she saw his receptionist and partner both leave for lunch before she let herself into his office.

True to his word, he was sitting behind his desk eating what looked like a wrap.

"On that low-carb diet?" she asked, lounging against the doorjamb as she watched him almost choke on the bite he'd just taken.

"Rose?" he managed to croak after chewing

and swallowing and quite possibly stalling for time to cover his initial startled reaction.

She didn't date a lot. She never went home with a man on the first date. Mike had been the exception, and at the time she'd had her reasons.

That was three months ago. Destiny or not, she'd been trying to put it behind her ever since. Which would have been easy if that night hadn't been wonderful. More than wonderful. And if Mike Flannigan hadn't kept calling, trying to get her to go out with him.

Their one night together, she'd left right after he'd fallen asleep. Had called a cab from outside and gone home to her own bed. He'd phoned the next day. She'd thanked him, but made it clear it had been a one-night thing. He'd called again a few times, asked her to dinner, suggested maybe they could date, suggested the one night together had meant more than she wanted to admit. She'd been tempted. Oh God, had she been tempted.

"It's been awhile," he said now, tossing the wrap into its plastic container and leaning back in his chair.

She had the feeling she'd just ruined his lunch. "I need to know why Jenna Dante hired you." It was a shot in the dark, but she saw she'd hit her target.

One brow shot up. Part of Mike Flannigan's appeal was his sense of humor. That and his blond good looks.

"You really think I'm going to tell you?" he asked with a disbelieving grin as she stepped into the room and closed the door behind her.

"Jenna's in trouble. Her ex paid me a visit this morning. It seems his plan was to take me for a ride. Judging by the gun he was holding, I don't think he planned to bring me back. He mentioned that he'd see both me and his ex in hell. She might already be dead for all I know. I'm hoping not. If she is still alive, I have to find her. Warn her."

"*Warn* her?" Mike studied Rose for a moment, his expression serious. He let out a curse. "You tried to get her to turn state's evidence and you think Lorenzo found out." It wasn't a question.

"She didn't know enough about Lorenzo's business, so I cut her loose." Rose glanced away, unable to meet his eyes. If Lorenzo had found out, then he'd gotten the information from someone in the department. It was no secret that Lorenzo had some pull down there.

Mike swore again. "As if Jenna Dante wasn't in enough trouble." He sounded angry with Rose. No more than she was with herself. But it had been her job to get close to Jenna Dante, find out if she could help put Lorenzo away. Rose should have known the department would pull off the officer keeping tabs on Jenna.

Rose met Mike's gaze, her chin going up as she straightened into her tough-gal cop persona. "We could do this the hard way. I could subpoena her file, have you thrown in jail if you don't give it up…." She stepped closer and placed both hands on his desk, leaning toward him. She could smell the wrap. Turkey and Swiss with cream cheese, avocado, sprouts. She would never have taken Mike for a sprouts man. "If she's still alive, I'm going to find her and help her. You going to make this easy for me?"

"I thought you were on medical leave," he said. "Something about a stab wound?"

He'd been keeping track of her? "It healed. My official leave unofficially ended this morning with Lorenzo's visit."

Mike shook his head and leaned back, studying her. "Lorenzo took the kid. There'd been other times when he'd 'forgotten' to return her after visitations. The police department gave him a warning. The court ordered that all visitations be supervised. So he swiped the kid from her bed in the middle of the night. He didn't even bother to hide. Just took the girl back to that estate where he and Jenna had lived together. He knew Jenna's hands were tied. The cops had backed off. The courts really couldn't protect her or her daughter. Not from a man like Lorenzo Dante. I offered to help her, but she wanted to do it on her own—"

It was Rose's turn to shake her head. "On her own against a man like Lorenzo?" What the hell had Jenna been thinking? Did she really believe she was any kind of match for a man like him? "Have you heard from her?"

Mike frowned. "She told me she'd send me a check. That was yesterday, the last time I talked to her."

"You should have gotten the money up front. I doubt the check is in the mail." Sarcasm went with the job. "I went by her apartment. Looks as if she took off. Or didn't return. Have any idea where she was going to go if she got her daughter back?"

He shook his head. "Run, I would imagine. If she got away. Otherwise…"

Otherwise she was dead. Rose studied Mike, wishing she could forget the night they'd spent together. She wondered if he remembered it the way she did. "If she calls, would you let me know?"

He rocked forward, his blue-eyed gaze locking with hers as he picked up a pen and notepad. "And you'll let me know what you learn?"

She nodded and gave him her cell phone number. He wrote it down, tore off the sheet of paper and folded it into a neat little square before sliding out his wallet and placing it inside.

When he finished, he settled his gaze on her as if waiting, letting her know he expected her to say something. Not about Jenna Dante. With their careers, they both dealt with the dark side of human nature on a daily basis.

Except Mike seemed to handle it better, seemed to find a way to distance himself from that part of his life—compartmentalize it so he could have more. That more, he'd told her, was a meaningful relationship based on love and friendship and hope.

Mike Flannigan thought he could have taught her how to make the two work, but she'd never given him the chance.

"I wish I'd gone out with you again, okay?" she said. "That night was—" she waved her hand through the air, meeting his gaze "—amazing."

He smiled as if that's all he'd been waiting to hear and, picking up his turkey-cheese wrap, leaned back in his chair.

She grinned at him, seeing that he knew how hard that had been for her to admit. "Thanks for the help."

"Good luck, Rose."

She would need more than luck and they both knew it. "You have my number."

He nodded. "Yeah, I do, don't I."

JENNA LOUNGED IN THE wonderfully hot water as her daughter splashed in the shallows next to her. The outdoor pools were just as Elmer had said: enchanting. Carved out among the rocks and trees, they wound like a creek along the edge of the mountainside, providing a natural landscape and at the same time intimacy.

Jenna tried to relax in the hot water, pushing away thoughts of her dream. She had more to worry about than some man in an old photograph or the thought that she was losing her mind. The duffel bag full of money in her room felt like a noose around her neck. She had to get it back to Lorenzo. She wasn't naive enough to think she could use it to buy her freedom. But she knew that Lorenzo was moving heaven and earth right now to find her, more so because of that stupid bag of money.

She had thought about calling him and telling him where he could pick it up. That was before she got trapped here.

No, she decided, it would be better for Lorenzo

to pick up the money at her apartment. She didn't want him knowing which direction she'd headed. With luck she wouldn't leave a trail he could follow—once she got him back the money.

"Look, Mommy!" Lexi called as she dipped her head under the water.

Jenna watched her through the steam, smiling and offering words of encouragement. All the time her mind was racing. Who could she trust to take the money to the apartment?

Only two people came to mind. She hated to ask either of them, afraid to involve them in her life—or worse, Lorenzo's. But if she did this right, Lorenzo would never know who'd put the cash in her apartment for him.

Once the money was on the way to her apartment, she could call him and tell him where to pick it up. He must be going crazy. He'd been too close to crazy as it was. Little things often set him off. This, she feared, was monumental.

Whatever she did, she had to make sure that Lexi was protected.

Lexi waved at someone at one of the other pools behind Jenna. Jenna feared it would be the imaginary woman in the purple plumed hat.

Bracing herself, she turned to look through the steam. She didn't see anyone. Nothing new there. That awful feeling began to settle in the pit of her stomach. "Who were you waving to?" she asked, fighting to keep the growing fear out of her voice.

"That man."

"Elmer. The nice man who gave us the room?"

Lexi shook her head. "The one with the funny hair on his lip."

Jenna's heart began to pound. "A man with a mustache?"

Lexi nodded and Jenna turned to look in the direction of the other pool, where Lexi had been gazing. "I don't see anyone." Her voice broke. "Is he still there?" she asked in a hoarse, scared whisper.

Lexi shook her head. "He's gone. I guess he didn't want you to see him."

Jenna couldn't breathe. "What do you mean?"

Lexi shrugged and bobbed up and down in the water, clearly losing interest in the conversation.

Fear compressed Jenna's chest, making it hard to catch her breath, let alone talk. "What did the man look like?"

Her daughter sighed, scrunching her face up in thought. She'd always been dramatic, using her hands and a variety of facial expressions when she talked. Now she let out a big sigh.

"Mommy," she said, throwing her arms wide,

NO POSTAGE
NECESSARY
IF MAILED
IN THE
UNITED STATES

BUSINESS REPLY MAIL

FIRST-CLASS MAIL   PERMIT NO. 717-003   BUFFALO, NY

POSTAGE WILL BE PAID BY ADDRESSEE

HARLEQUIN READER SERVICE
3010 WALDEN AVE
PO BOX 1867
BUFFALO NY 14240-9952

Get FREE BOOKS and a FREE GIFT when you play the...

LAS VEGAS GAME

Just scratch off the gold box with a coin. Then check below to see the gifts you get!

YES! I have scratched off the gold box. Please send me my **2 FREE BOOKS** and **gift for which I qualify**. I understand that I am under no obligation to purchase any books as explained on the back of this card.

382 HDL D7ZX   182 HDL D7XZ

FIRST NAME	LAST NAME

ADDRESS

APT.#	CITY

STATE/PROV.	ZIP/POSTAL CODE

(H-I-10/05)

7	7	7	Worth TWO FREE BOOKS plus a BONUS Mystery Gift!
🍒	🍒	🍒	Worth TWO FREE BOOKS!
🔔	🔔	♣	TRY AGAIN!

www.eHarlequin.com

"he just looked like a *man*." She frowned as if she'd thought of something. "He was wearing funny clothes and his hair was wet."

"Wet?" Jenna thought of the photograph of the man in the tuxedo. His hair was oiled and combed straight back.

Lexi ducked under the water again, and despite the warmth of the hot springs, Jenna shivered. It wasn't possible that Lexi had seen the man.

They had to get out of this place. Get the money to Lorenzo. Then she would take Lexi as far from here as possible.

"Did you see me go all the way to the bottom?" Lexi asked, bobbing up again.

"I saw," Jenna managed to say.

"Wanna see me swim?" Lexi didn't wait for an answer. She took off, paddling wildly, sending spray in all directions, then stopped to grin back at her mother. "Did you see?"

Jenna nodded and smiled, her heart a hammer. She tried to convince herself that she shouldn't be scared, that this was only a very imaginative, bright little girl. But she remembered how Lexi used to scare Lorenzo by seeming old for her age—and wise beyond her years.

Her preschool teachers said she was gifted.

Or maybe she just has the gift.

"Lexi, it's time to go." Upset and shaking, Jenna started to get out of the pool.

"No, not yet, Mommy!"

Weak from the hot water and her fears, Jenna let herself slip back into the water. "A few more minutes, but then no arguments, agreed?"

Lexi grudgingly nodded.

Jenna sank neck deep in the water, feeling cold now. Why had she thought these pools, this place, at all enchanting?

HARRY BALLANTINE WATCHED Jenna and her daughter through the steam rising off the pool, shaken.

The little girl had *seen* him. How was that possible? No one had seen him in seventy years. He'd been in a vaporous limbo, drifting in the wind. Nothing. Absolutely nothing.

Until the woman and child had arrived last night from out of the rain and darkness and he'd gone to the window. Was it possible the woman had seen him, too? She'd looked up as if knowing he was there.

My God, it was the first time anyone had seen him—let alone felt his touch. Did he dare hope?

He moved toward the pools, half-afraid.

The woman was in a deeper end of a pool, not

far from her daughter. Her eyes were closed, but he could tell she was listening to the little girl chattering away to herself nearby.

He watched the woman brush a strand of dark hair back from her face. She really was lovely. High cheekbones, porcelain smooth skin, dark fringed lashes. There was an innocence about her that pulled at something deep within him.

You are beautiful, Jenna.

She stirred, her eyes coming open as if she'd heard him.

Can you hear me?

Her dark eyes widened and she looked around.

My God, she *could* hear him.

Don't be afraid. I won't hurt you.

He was so close now that he could see she was trembling.

Remember last night?

The pulse at her throat began to pound. She reached for the side of the pool as she tried to find bottom.

"Lexi, we have to go now." Her words came out choked with fear.

No, please don't leave.

"Mommy, it's not time. You said we could stay for a little while longer," Lexi cried. "Please, just a few more minutes. Please."

He touched Jenna's shoulder and she froze, eyes wide with terror—and something else he recognized. Need.

SHE WAS LOSING HER MIND.
I'm here. It's all right.

She let out the breath she'd been holding. It came with a sob, and she dropped back into the water, suddenly too weak to pull herself out.

His voice was velvet. And familiar. She'd heard it last night in her dreams and had known it was the voice of the man in the old photograph.

She stared into the steam rising from the surface of the pool, knowing no one was out there and yet at the same time bracing herself for his touch, yearning for it, feeling terrified that, like the voice, it would be familiar.

"I can't…" She tried to climb out of the pool, but something pulled her back down.
You don't have to go yet.

She felt hysterical laughter bubbling up. "This isn't happening."
Yes, it is.

She sucked in a breath as she felt him pull her back down to him. She closed her eyes, telling herself this wasn't real. But it felt more real than anything she'd ever experienced.

"Tell me I'm not losing my mind," she whispered.

You're not. I'm here.

Her body revved up like an engine taking off. "If you knew what I was thinking…"

She heard a soft chuckle. *Don't I?*

She could feel him under the water, his touch cool. Familiar.

Sometimes things are exactly as they seem.

She shook her head, unable to accept that this was happening. How could she have feelings toward…what? A man from a seventy-year-old photograph? Or something else?

"Who are you?" she whispered, feeling tears well in her eyes as she pulled free of him. "W*hat* are you?"

You know me.

"No." She didn't know him. But she sensed things about him. Both good—and bad.

"Mommy, look!" Lexi called, breaking the spell.

Jenna jerked free and reached for the side of the pool. In an instant she had pulled herself out. "Lexi, come on. We have to go. *Now.*"

From the shallow end of the pool the little girl started to protest, but Jenna hurried toward her, drawing her out. Holding her hand, she moved quickly to their towels.

It wasn't until she'd covered herself and Lexi that she turned to look back.

But of course there was no one there.

Chapter Nine

Jenna scooped Lexi up into her arms and ran toward the lobby, praying that Elmer had returned.

"How did you like the swimming pool, little lady?" he said, smiling at her daughter. His gaze shifted to Jenna and his expression changed. "You saw them."

Her heart dropped. *"Them?"*

"I'm sorry but I didn't want to say anything to scare you, but I've felt them. Even saw one. Some old gal in a purple hat with feathers."

"She's nice," Lexi said. "She waved and smiled at me."

Jenna drew her daughter closer as she stared at Elmer. "You're telling me…"

He nodded. "From what I could learn, she was the hotel owner's wife. She was—" he glanced at Lexi "—lost opening night in 1936."

In the fire. Jenna took a ragged breath, her gaze going to the photograph of the man from her dream. "What do you know about Bobby John Chamberlain?" she asked, motioning toward the picture.

Elmer stepped closer and frowned. "Bobby John Chamberlain." He reached under the counter, then stopped, his frown deepening.

"What's wrong?" she asked.

"There was a box of Fernhaven pamphlets under here. They seem to be gone." He looked confused and a little scared.

"Maybe you moved them and didn't remember," she said, wondering why it mattered. She'd obviously rattled the poor man.

"It's just…odd. But you're right, I probably moved them. Or someone else did yesterday and I didn't notice." He didn't sound convinced, but he seemed to shake it off as he reached under the registration desk and brought out a stack of photographs. He went through them, mumbling to himself, obviously still agitated over the missing box of pamphlets.

"The owners of the hotel got photographs from the newspaper archive," Elmer said. "A lot of the photos ran after the fire. It was big news as you can imagine."

Jenna held her breath as he drew out a photo and handed it to her. Like the other photo, the name Bobby John Chamberlain had a line through it, with "Harry Ballantine" neatly printed underneath in different handwriting.

"Who is Harry Ballantine?" she asked, afraid she didn't want to know.

Elmer nodded as if to himself. "I looked up some of those old newspaper articles from June 1936. It's funny you should ask about Harry Ballantine. There were a lot of famous people at Fernhaven that night. But Harry was without a doubt the most infamous. He was a renowned jewel thief in his day."

"A *thief*," Jenna said, wondering why she would be surprised. She'd married Lorenzo, hadn't she? Why not conjure up a jewel thief for a phantom lover? "Why was the other name under his photo?"

"The story came out after the tragedy that Harry had conned a rich Texan oilman named Bobby John Chamberlain out of his invitation to the 1936 Fernhaven grand opening."

"What happened to Harry?" she asked, her voice barely recognizable even to her own ears.

"Died in the fire. Ironic, isn't it? If he hadn't stolen the Chamberlain fellow's identity, he wouldn't have died. But then again, he was a thief, no doubt here to steal some of that jewelry in those photographs." Elmer sighed. "In a way, I guess he got his just rewards. Strange, though, how Chamberlain died right after that. An accident at one of his oil rigs. I guess he just couldn't beat death."

Jenna was speechless. Her pulse pounded in her ears, a deafening drumming. Her limbs felt weak as water. She stared down at the photograph of Harry Ballantine, a man she felt she knew. Dead for seventy years…

"He the one you're seeing?" Elmer asked.

She shook her head. "I didn't see anything."

Elmer nodded knowingly. "With the rain stopped, the highway patrol said they should have the road open sometime later today. I left a breakfast tray outside the door to your room."

"Thank you."

"They can't hurt you or your daughter," Elmer said. "You're safe here."

Jenna wasn't so sure about that.

ONCE INSIDE THE ROOM, Jenna locked the door behind them and stood for a moment trying to get her heart rate back down. She was shaking, and not from the cold.

Fred came out Lexi's bedroom meowing loudly.

Jenna started toward her own bedroom and stopped. Someone had been in the room. She sniffed the air. That scent. She'd smelled it last night in the dream.

Unnerved, she tried to convince herself she'd only imagined it. Just as she'd imagined the voice, the feel of the man in the pool. Her body still tingled from the feel of him against her in the hot water. Harry Ballantine? Thief?

She thought of the duffel bag of money and raced into the bedroom. It was where she'd left it, and none of the money appeared to be missing.

She rezipped the bag, shoved it into the back of the closet and sat down heavily on the bed.

In the other room Lexi was talking to Clarice and eating the breakfast Elmer had sent up. From the doorway Fred was meowing loudly, as if trying to tell Jenna what had taken place while she'd been gone.

She tried to pull herself together. After a few moments she realized that Fred had gone into Lexi's room and was acting almost normal. Almost too normal for a cat. When she glanced into her daughter's room, she found Lexi was rubbing her eyes.

"Come here, sweetheart."

Lexi stumbled to her and let Jenna hold her.

"Why don't we lie down for a little while?"

Lexi nodded sleepily against her.

Jenna helped her daughter out of her swimsuit and into warm, dry clothing. When she tucked her into the bed, Lexi was asleep in an instant. Playing in the hot water, plus the interrupted sleep from last night, had tired them both out.

Unable to put it off any longer, Jenna left Lexi's bedroom door open and went to her own room to retrieve her cell phone. She hesitated. The road would be open soon. And the instant it was, she was getting out. She had to trust someone. Someone who would help her.

She was in short supply of friends. Lorenzo had seen to that. She couldn't call Raymond Valencia and ask for more help.

He'd helped her all through the divorce, even telling her who to contact to get fake passports. But she couldn't involve him again. She'd seen the way he looked at her.

Asking for his help again would only open her up to something she wasn't interested in pursuing—and possibly put her in more danger. Fortunately she'd met two women since she'd moved out and gotten the divorce. Charlene Palmer lived in the same apartment house as Jenna. She'd met the other woman, Rose Garcia, in the grocery store. They'd since run into each other at the park.

Jenna thought of the two women, both so different. Neither knew Lorenzo, or vice versa.

Jenna flushed at the memory of how she'd confided in both women, complete strangers. She'd been raised to keep her personal business to herself, and yet she'd opened up to Rose especially. Rose had been so easy to talk to. While Jenna had never mentioned Lorenzo's name, she'd told her new friend everything that had happened.

Even now she wondered why she'd done that, knowing how dangerous it was to talk to anyone.

But Rose had been so supportive and such a good listener. And Jenna had thought she'd never see her again.

As it was, she'd run into her on a half-dozen occasions. Rose had encouraged her to go to the police with what she knew, to try to put Lorenzo behind bars. Jenna had assured her she knew nothing about Lorenzo's business affairs, and shuddered at the thought of what her ex-husband would have done if she'd gone to the authorities.

"He has some of the police on his payroll," Jenna had told her.

Rose had been shocked and wanted to know who.

"I don't know. I just know that when I went to the police when he ignored the court's orders, nothing happened."

"He thinks he's above the law, but he's not," Rose had argued.

Jenna had laughed. "He *is* above the law. His power extends far beyond the police, believe me. He's a ruthless man who destroys anyone who gets in his way."

"Let me help you," Rose had insisted, pressing a piece of paper with her cell phone number on it into Jenna's hand.

Jenna had hidden the number in her purse, but she'd never called. No one understood just how dangerous Lorenzo Dante was. And she didn't want to drag anyone else into this.

Her other new friend was her neighbor, Charlene Palmer. She'd met Charlene one day after Lorenzo had broken the restraining order and come by, making loud threats and breaking things. Fortunately, Lexi had been in an afternoon preschool program up the street.

Charlene had come over right after Lorenzo left, and had asked if she could help. The walls were thin; she'd obviously heard everything.

Charlene was a large, soft woman with a kind face. She'd given Jenna a hug, gone into the kitchen and poured them both diet colas, then sat down and said, "Talk to me, honey. That bastard who was just here—your ex, right?" She hadn't waited for an answer. She'd just started telling Jenna about her own ex, who she said was doing time in prison.

Jenna had worried at first about befriending Charlene. Not that Charlene would have any reason to know who Lorenzo was. It wasn't as if he'd ever been arrested for his crimes and gotten his picture in the paper. And Jenna had rented the apartment in her maiden name, McDonald.

It seemed safe to talk to a woman who seemed to actually understand because she'd been in her shoes.

And Jenna liked Charlene. The woman had survived misfortune, was easygoing, had an attitude Jenna admired.

It had been Charlene's idea to keep Jenna's spare apartment key. "Honey, I had a husband like your ex. He beat me up so bad one night…" Tears had welled in Charlene's eyes. She'd brushed at them angrily. "Thank God I'd given my apartment key to a friend who lived next door. She waited until my old man left, then came over and took me to the hospital. I would have bled to death on the floor if she hadn't had a key. In our neighborhood you didn't call the cops. And you couldn't afford an ambulance."

The story had chilled Jenna. Lorenzo was capable of hurting her. Hurting her badly.

Jenna knew that either woman would help her. She pulled out her purse.

She dialed a number. It rang once, twice, three times. Jenna started to hang up, suddenly afraid she'd picked the wrong person to trust.

CHARLENE PALMER HAD HER feet up on the coffee table, a bag of potato chips on one side of her and a box of cookies on the other. She'd just poured herself a large glass of diet cola and had settled in to watch her favorite soap. Life was good.

Her cell phone rang in her purse on the other side of the room. She eyed it suspiciously. It rang again. She swore softly. Her show was just starting, and when the phone rang it was never good news.

It rang a third time. And she had the oddest feeling that she should answer it. She shoved herself up from the couch and launched herself across the room, snatching up her purse, digging deep and coming up with the phone as it rang a fourth time.

"Yeah?" She was out of breath, heart pounding from the exertion of just crossing the room.

Plus it always spooked her a little when she got one of those "feelings." Her Grandmother Tyler believed she could see the future. Of course, everyone in the family thought her just a crazy old bat.

But one time Grandmother Tyler had stared into Charlene's eyes and said, "You got the gift, too, don't you, girl?"

Charlene had denied it. Hell, she didn't need that kind of gift. No way.

And yet even before she heard Jenna Dante's voice, Charlene knew that her "gift" hadn't let her down—at least not this time. Answering this call was the smartest thing she'd done in a long time.

"Charlene?"

Jenna Dante. She tried to catch her breath. "Hey, girl." She felt a sharp stab of regret as she hit the TV's mute button. She hated missing her show. "You all right?" Jenna hadn't come home last night and she'd been worried about her.

"You said if I ever needed help…"

Charlene looked toward the heavens and smiled at her luck. "I meant it. What can I do?" She glanced at her soap ruefully and just hoped nothing big happened on it today.

"I'm kind of in a bind," Jenna said on the other end of the line.

"It's that ex of yours, isn't it," Charlene stated.

"I'm afraid so. I have something of his I didn't mean to take. Now I need to get it back to him," Jenna explained.

Something of her ex's? Charlene held her breath.

"The thing is, this package that I need to get to my ex, I can't mail it."

Charlene let out the breath she'd been holding. "We're not talking drugs here, right?"

"No, no, nothing like that," Jenna said quickly. "It's just some papers I didn't mean to take." She sighed. "It's a long story. But I thought if I could get them to my apartment, I could call him and tell him where to pick them up." She paused. "You know, maybe this wasn't such a good idea."

Papers. Right. "Look, are you sure you shouldn't go to the cops? What am I saying? You already went to them. They can't protect you from him. Hey, I can get him the papers. Just tell me where to pick them up."

Silence. For a moment Charlene was afraid Jenna had hung up.

"Charlene, I'm not in Seattle. It's too far and you can't—"

"Hey, what are friends for? And it's not like I'm doing anything." She glanced wistfully at her soap opera. "I've even got wheels. A friend sold me her used car when she traded up." A small lie. At least for the moment. "And I'm up for a road trip. What else do I have to do? Just tell me how to get to you."

"Are you sure?"

"Absolutely." Charlene found a pen and turned over one of the bill envelopes on her coffee table. "Just give me directions."

"Well, there is one small problem," Jenna said, and explained about the bridge and the flooding.

"I'm sure I'll be able to get through by the time I reach there," Charlene said.

"It will be good to see you."

JENNA AND FRANCO. Lorenzo couldn't believe how well this was all working out. Not that he could see Jenna with Franco. Not in a million years. But if Valencia found Jenna first, then he would find her with the duffel bag full of money. What else would he think? No matter what she said, Valencia wouldn't believe her.

And if Lorenzo managed to find Jenna first?

Little chance of that happening. Alfredo hadn't been able to locate her. Jenna could be miles from here by now. But didn't that mean Valencia wouldn't be able to trace her, either?

Lorenzo breathed a sigh of relief. He couldn't have planned this better.

His cell phone rang. He flipped it open, stared at the caller ID and smiled. Lady luck was shining on him today. "Yeah?"

"Mr. Dante?" said the female voice. There was a mocking lilt to the way she said the mister that he didn't like.

"Charlene," he said, and waited. The last time she'd called it was to tell him that Jenna had taken off. By that time, he'd already figured it out. He had wondered why Charlene hadn't phoned sooner with the information. Wasn't that what he was paying her for?

"I just heard from Jenna," she said into the silence.

Well, maybe setting Charlene Palmer up in the same apartment complex to spy on his ex-wife hadn't been such a bad idea, after all. Charlene had befriended Jenna, as she'd been hired to do. But up until this minute, she hadn't given him anything that had been worth her rent, let alone paying all her expenses so she could sit around on her butt.

"She wants me to meet her," Charlene said. "I told her I have a car."

Lorenzo's smile faded. "A car?"

"How else could I meet her?"

She was holding out for a *car?* He thought about driving over to the apartment complex and showing her how he felt about extortion.

Charlene hadn't been wild about doing his bidding to begin with. But what choice did she have, with her brother in prison? Stan Palmer had worked for Lorenzo until he got caught hijacking a semi load of electronics. Lorenzo had the ability to make Stan's life in prison even less enjoyable if Charlene didn't do what Lorenzo wanted.

"A car," he said again. "What kind of car?"

"A newer model used one," Charlene said.

"Not a *brand-new* one?" He couldn't keep the sarcasm out of his voice.

She chuckled. "Now what would a woman like me be doing with a fancy new car?"

"Where is my ex-wife?" he snapped, tired of this.

"She says she has something that she took by mistake and wants to return to you. Some…papers? I'm to pick up the package as soon as I get a car and drive to where she is."

His *money.* Jenna wanted to return his money? He shook his head in amazement. She *did* have a brain. Not that returning his money was going to save her. If she thought that, then she was out of her mind.

And no way was he letting Charlene Palmer within a mile of that duffel bag. He'd never see her or the money or his newer model used car again. "I'll meet her. Just give me the address."

"It isn't going down that way. If anyone else comes, she'll skip and you can forget whatever it is she took from you," Charlene said. "You want it back? Then we do this her way."

Lorenzo gripped the cell phone so hard he heard it crack. "Do you have any idea who you're dealing with?" he demanded.

"Oh, yeah," Charlene said with another chuckle. "And so does your ex. I have to wonder why she would give you anything back. Must be pretty important."

Lorenzo swore under his breath. "If I have to come over there—"

"You really think I'd still be here?" There was a sound as if she was starting to hang up.

"Wait!" He gritted his teeth until his jaw ached. "We'll do it your way. I'll get you a car. You make the pickup. I'll have the title signed over in your name as soon as you give me the package and her location." Silence. "And I give you five thousand dollars to end our business arrangement."

"Make it twenty thousand, you put the title of the car in my name right away and I give you the location after I make the pickup."

He would kill her when this was over. "How do I know I can trust you?"

"You don't. Make it a red car. I like red. Something nice. Don't be cheap. You'll probably want to have it delivered as soon as possible so I can get going. Jenna isn't anywhere near Seattle. I'll call you on my cell phone when I have the package, and we can set up an exchange. I'd like that twenty grand in new bills."

He cursed the turn his life had taken. Women were now calling the shots? He'd been beaten up and hog-tied by a woman, his ex-wife had stolen his daughter and his money, and now this woman was telling him how things were going to be?

"You do realize the fine line you are walking here?" he asked Charlene in his most calm voice.

She chuckled. "I have nothing to lose. How about you?" She let out a long sigh. "The sooner I get the car, the sooner I get your *papers* back." She hung up.

He threw the cell phone across the room and immediately regretted it as the phone shattered in a spray of plastic. He'd have to buy not only a car but also a new cell phone.

Picking up the land line, he first called Alfredo, then a car dealer and ordered a car delivered to Charlene's address, the title in her name, plus a cash payment to be made from his bank account. The only red car the dealer had was going to set him back over ten grand. Lorenzo swore and told the dealer that the car had to be delivered immediately.

The doorbell rang.

"Screw the paperwork. Put the insurance under my name then. Just get the car to that address *now,*" he barked into the phone, having to raise his voice because of the sudden pounding at the front door. "What the hell?" Lorenzo swore. He hung up and went to the door to look out.

Cops?

RAYMOND VALENCIA HAD SENT Jolly and Rico over to Jenna Dante's apartment after numerous attempts to reach her had failed. They came back with the bad news.

"Looks like she skipped," Rico said, playing with the toothpick in his mouth. "Super said she left last night and didn't come back."

"How the hell does the apartment super know that?" Raymond snapped.

"Insomniac. Saw her leave with two suitcases, a large one and a small one. Seemed to be in a hurry. Her parking space was empty all night. No sign of her this morning."

Raymond pulled on his left earlobe, a habit when he was thinking. "No one has any idea where she went?"

Rico shook his head.

"And what about this Rose Garcia woman? Any word on her?"

Jolly shrugged. "Lorenzo scared her off."

It always came back to Lorenzo.

Rico pulled the toothpick from his mouth. "After a little persuasion, we found out that someone else had been snooping around the apartment." He paused as if waiting for a drum roll. "Some broad," he said finally, nodding and smiling. "A cop. Name was Rose Garcia."

Raymond stared at Rico, his mind reeling at the implications. He tried not to show his surprise. Or his distress at the news. A cop looking for Jenna. A cop whose number was on Franco's cell phone. Nothing about this situation boded well.

Was Franco working with the cops?

Or worse, was Franco a cop? If so, he'd certainly fooled him. Raymond had always prided himself on his instincts. If he was wrong about Franco, could he also be wrong about Jenna? If so, how did she fit into the picture?

"Tell me something," Raymond said after a moment. "You knew Franco. Can you see him with Jenna Dante?"

Rico laughed. "That broad was too classy for *Dante,* let alone a dunce like Franco. No way."

Raymond wanted to argue that Franco was no dunce. There had been intelligence behind all that attitude. In fact, Franco could have been smarter than Raymond had realized. He'd certainly fooled him. Raymond looked to Jolly. "What do you think?"

"I don't know, Boss. I've *never* understood women."

Rico laughed and even Raymond had to smile.

"I know what you mean, Jolly," Raymond said. "I've never understood women, either." But he'd thought he'd understood Jenna. He'd thought he knew her. More important, he'd thought he could trust her. Just as he had Franco.

Now he wasn't so sure. "You left a man watching Jenna Dante's apartment and another one watching Lorenzo?" Both nodded. "Rico, I want you on Lorenzo. You know the drill." Rico nodded. "Jolly, you take the apartment. I want to know if anyone comes or goes. *Anyone.*"

Rico's cell rang. He checked the caller ID,

looked at his boss, then quickly answered. "Yeah. No kiddin'. Yeah." He snapped it off. "The guy I left at Dante's. He just called to say that cops are there. Had a warrant and everything. Got one of them forensics teams in there. And two detectives just took Dante downtown in handcuffs."

Raymond Valencia swore. Hadn't he known he would live to regret not killing Lorenzo?

DETECTIVE ROSE GARCIA cupped the cell phone to her ear as her fingers whipped over the computer keyboard at a Ballard Internet café.

"We got a warrant to search Dante's house, and picked up blood spatters in the tile grout on the living room floor," Detective Luke Henry said on the other end of the line.

"Franco's?" she asked scared.

"Maybe. Could be his ex's. Got the forensics guy on it and Dante in custody. He says the blood is from a cut on his hand. Has a fresh cut. Unless we find more evidence of foul play, we aren't going to be able to hold him, and he knows it."

Rose stopped typing and closed her eyes.

"You still there?"

She took a breath, opened her eyes. "Let's say he did the ex. Where's the daughter?"

"We found a bedroom upstairs. Had some little girl's clothes in it. Dante says he has visitation rights. Doesn't get the daughter again until the weekend. Claims he hasn't seen or heard from his ex since the last time he had supervised visitation."

"He's lying."

Luke laughed. "You think? But unless we have a body…"

"Yeah. I'm running her credit card right now to see if she's used it in the last twenty-four hours. Maybe we'll get lucky." Maybe by some miracle Jenna Dante had escaped her ex-husband. "Still no word from Franco?"

"No. Shouldn't you be home taking it easy?"

"I'm fine. It was just a little knife wound. The perp barely cut me. It wasn't like he shot me." She snapped her cell phone shut and stared at the computer screen.

Jenna hadn't used her credit card late last night. Rose felt a wave of disappointment. Now what?

Unable not to think about the blood Luke had found at Dante's house, Rose checked the police wire. If Lorenzo had dumped the bodies, maybe they'd been found by now.

One report caught her eye. A woman and child and elderly security guard had been stranded at an empty hotel in the Cascades. Highway patrol were unable to reach the three, but had talked to the security guard on the phone.

But what had caught Rose's eye was the model and color of the SUV the woman had been driving, information provided by the security guard. It matched one owned by Lorenzo Dante. But now that Rose thought about it, she realized Dante hadn't been driving it this morning when he'd almost hit her.

She called Luke. "Is Lorenzo Dante's black SUV out there?"

"No, hold on." Luke left the line and came back. "He says it was stolen. He hasn't had time to report it yet. He's driving a rental, and guess whose car is parked out back?"

"Jenna's," Rose said. "Bingo. I think she took his SUV, for whatever reason. If I'm right, I might be able to find her."

"Rose? Listen, I don't want you doing anything without backup, and there is no way I can back you up with you being on medical leave, do you hear me?"

"I won't do anything without backup. I promise."

She hung up. Her instincts told her she was on the right track. If Lorenzo Dante's SUV really had been stolen, he would have called the cops right away in a fury. But if Jenna had taken it…

Rose jotted down the name of the place. Fernhaven Hotel.

Opening her bottom desk drawer, she pulled out a map of Washington State. Based on the police report, she found the approximate location of the hotel. About two hours from Seattle.

She crossed her fingers as she dialed directory assistance and got the number for the hotel. But when she called the phone rang and rang, each ring causing her more concern. Rose couldn't shake the feeling that the woman and child stranded at the hotel were Jenna Dante, now McDonald, and her daughter, Alexandria—and that they were in more trouble than they realized.

As the phone rang, Rose studied the map. No close towns around, and according to the latest update, no way in. The highway was flooded to the east and impassable, and a bridge was out to the west.

Still no answer. She let it ring until it was picked up by voice mail. The message informed her that the hotel wasn't open for business but would be taking reservations next week, and that a grand opening was scheduled three weeks out.

She would keep trying the number. In the

meantime, there had to be a way to get to Fernhaven. That country was crisscrossed with old logging roads. Not the kind of route she could drive in a Mini Cooper, but she knew someone who had a Jeep—and she did need backup.

She dialed Mike Flannigan's number.

Chapter Ten

Jenna was still trembling after her phone call to Charlene. She had tried to convince herself she'd done the right thing. But now she feared she had only managed to put Charlene's life in danger.

And all to get the money back to Lorenzo.

Maybe she shouldn't have even tried. Would it really make that much difference? Something told her it did. No way would Lorenzo have that kind of money just lying around in a duffel bag in the back of the SUV. Especially since he was planning to fly out the next day. He would never have gotten that bag of money through customs.

So what had he planned to do with it?

Since she'd returned to the room, she hadn't heard any voices in her head. Maybe she'd never heard voices. Or felt someone in the pool with her.

Stress did strange things to a person. And with

Lorenzo out there somewhere looking for her…well, no wonder odd things were happening to her.

She shivered at the memory and realized she was still wearing her swimsuit and wrap. Going into the bathroom, she turned on the water and stripped out of her wet clothing. To keep her mind busy she went over the phone conversation with Charlene again in her head.

Charlene had been so understanding. "Honey, the best thing you can do is get out of the country as soon as possible, right? You wouldn't have run unless you thought you had to, and I got to tell you, some bad-looking guys have been coming around hunting for you. Whatever it is that you accidentally took, give it back. Hell, you don't want any more trouble from that man."

Jenna knew Charlene was right. "You'll make sure you aren't followed," she'd said.

"Don't worry. Your ex doesn't know me from Adam. I'll be on my way within the hour," Charlene had assured her. "It will be great to see you, too. And don't worry, I'm sure the road will be open by then."

Had she made the right choice, calling Charlene for help? Jenna prayed so as she soaped her body. She found herself listening for him. Just the thought brought on an ache that was both physical and emotional.

She shook it off as she climbed out of the tub and pulled on the warm guest robe. Then she froze.

He was *here*. She could feel him in the room. Her heart lodged in her throat. "Who are you?" she whispered hoarsely as she stepped back, grabbing the wall for support.

She stared in horror at the steamed-up mirror over the sink as letters began to slowly appear.

HARRY BALLANTINE

RAYMOND VALENCIA HAD BEEN waiting by the phone. Jolly had called to say that the cops were still searching Lorenzo Dante's house. Jolly thought they may have found something.

"Let me know when Lorenzo returns," Raymond said, ruing the day he'd ever met Lorenzo. What had the fool done? Something bad enough that Lorenzo might try to make a deal to save his sorry self?

Raymond had hoped it wouldn't come to this, but clearly Lorenzo would have to be dealt with. Unfortunately, now that the police were involved, it would have to be done with some finesse. That left out Jolly and Rico.

"There is something I thought you'd want to know," Jolly said. "Her car is here."

"Whose car?" Raymond asked impatiently.

"Mrs. Dante's."

"*Jenna's?* Is she there?"

"I dunno. Doesn't seem to be. Cops are crawling all over the place and the only other person I've seen is Lorenzo. But her car is parked out back. The police just got through searching it. A towing company came to take it away, but the cops stopped them."

Raymond swore under his breath. "Let me know the minute Lorenzo returns." He hung up.

The phone rang. More bad news?

"You said to call if anything unusual was going on," Rico said without preamble. "Well, it's probably nothing, but the local car dealer just dropped off a nice red Mustang for one of the tenants."

"That's nice, Rico, but not exactly—"

"I wouldn't mention it, but guess who took ownership?"

Raymond wasn't in the mood for guessing games.

"Stan Palmer's sister. Stan, the guy who got sent up for jacking that semi a couple of years ago? The guy who used to work for Dante?"

"Stan Palmer's sister lives in the same apartment house as Jenna Dante?" Raymond asked in astonishment. What were the chances of that in a city the size of Seattle?

"I recognize Charlene from one time when I picked Stan up for a job back when we were both freelancing," Rico said. "You think she knows Dante's ex-broad?"

What were the chances Charlene Palmer *didn't* know Jenna Dante, he wanted to demand of Rico.

"The dealer just handed her the keys," Rico said. "She's all excited about the car, like it's a present, you know?"

Raymond knew.

"Last I heard, Charlene couldn't afford bus fare and was living at the women's shelter. Her lack of looks aside, she's too nasty toward men to have found herself a sugar daddy."

Hadn't Rico been around long enough to realize that not all men wanted sex from a woman?

"She went back inside after signing the papers for the car," Rico said.

"Go in and ask the super who's been paying her rent. Persuade him to tell you," Raymond said. "Then call me right back. Make sure she doesn't leave before you come out again."

"You got it." Rico hung up.

Raymond waited by the phone. He knew he wouldn't have to wait long. Rico had excellent persuasion skills.

"You sitting down?" Rico said without preamble.

"Just tell me," Raymond said through gritted teeth.

"Paid through a corporation called L.D. Inc.," Rico said. "The super gets a kickback for keeping his mouth shut."

Raymond let out a curse. L.D. Inc. "Lorenzo Dante."

"You got it. Hey, Charlene just came back down. She's carrying a bag, like an overnight bag. Should I stop her?"

"No. Follow her," Raymond said. "Don't lose her. Call me as soon as she gets where she's going." He hung up, wondering what the hell was going on.

JENNA FLED THE BATHROOM and would have fled the hotel if she could have.

Lexi was sleeping soundly, with Fred curled next to her, purring, and Clarice snugged under one arm.

Jenna closed her daughter's bedroom door. There was no place to run. Charlene was on her way to pick up the money for Lorenzo. Jenna couldn't leave here even if the roads were open.

She glanced toward her own bedroom, afraid to go back in there. Afraid the letters would still be on the bathroom mirror.

Outside, the day had darkened with the promise of more rain. *No.* She couldn't stay trapped here much longer or she feared she would completely lose her mind. If she hadn't already.

She turned on all the lights in the living room to chase away the shadows and the threat of a storm outside. Then she curled up on the couch, wrapping the robe tightly around her, determined to fight the voice in her head.

But it was silent.

Her eyelids grew heavy from lack of sleep last night, from the hot water of the pool and the shower. She felt herself drifting, and tried to fight it, afraid he would be waiting for her, her defenses down.

And yet a part of her knew he would come the moment she fell asleep. She drifted off, waiting for him, yearning for him the way she'd never yearned for anyone before.

HARRY WASN'T EVEN AWARE that he'd touched her. Not until Jenna let out the smallest of sighs. He wished he could show himself to her. But even now he didn't understand how he'd been able to connect even this much with her. It was as if after seventy years something had come alive in him.

He focused his energies on his hands, not wanting his touch to be cold. He didn't want to repel her. He brushed a caress over her temple again, then across her cheek to her jaw. She stretched, arching her neck a little as he skimmed his now warm fingers down the slim column of her throat. She let out a low moan as his fingers stopped at the opening of her robe.

She rolled over on her back on the couch, stirred a little, then dropped back to sleep. He waited before he touched her again, waited until she was in a deep slumber. When he knew she would welcome him. She needed him as much as he did her.

His fingers went to the hollow just below her throat. He could feel her quickened pulse as he traced a path down between her full breasts. Her skin felt like fine silk, rich and lush and creamy smooth.

She smelled of the expensive soap from the shower. He breathed her in, moving closer as he concentrated on making his body warm. He slipped his hand under the opening at the top of the robe.

She shivered as he cupped one breast, being careful to do it slowly, tenderly. She moaned and turned her head away from him as she pressed her breast into his warm hand. The nipple hardened against his palm. How he ached to suck it into his mouth, to lave it with his tongue, to taste her skin, to kiss her warm flesh.

Carefully he untied her robe and let each side fall away from her body. Her nipples were rock hard, dark pink against her fair skin. He thumbed one, then the other as she arched against his touch and groaned in her sleep. Her skin was hot to the touch and her breathing short and fast.

What surprised him was his own reaction. He was aroused and he wanted this woman. He'd never wanted anything as much as he did her.

But as he looked down into her face, he knew there was something else going on here. Something Harry Ballantine could no more figure out than he could free himself from the hold she had on him, a hold she'd had from the moment he saw her come up the mountain to Fernhaven.

His fingers trailed down the flat of her stomach. She froze, and for a moment he thought she would awaken and be afraid again. He waited before he slipped his fingers over the slightly rounded mound to gently caress her. She didn't wake up. But she did respond, arching against his fingers, groaning once more as he skillfully took her higher and higher, her breath coming hard and fast, her body convulsing with pleasure until he took her to a climactic peak. She shuddered and sighed. All tension washed from her face. A slight smile curved her lips.

He drew the robe back over her as she turned onto her side again. Then he lay down beside her as if he, too, had been sated, he, too, had been released.

As Harry listened to her breathe, his heart ached. Only one of them would be leaving this place.

"ANY IDEA WHERE WE ARE?" Mike Flannigan asked as he shifted the Jeep into four-wheel drive. Ahead Rose could see nothing but trees, with a narrow slash cut through them that looked nothing like a road.

Mike had already had to stop numerous times to get out and move a small downed tree. Or find another way around larger fallen trees.

She looked down at the map in her lap and the compass Mike had given her. "We're going in the right direction, kinda."

He laughed and looked over at her.

She felt her heart jump in her chest and wished she hadn't gotten him involved in this. "This might have been a mistake."

"You think?" He shook his head as he reached over to lay his warm palm on her shoulder. "We'll find the road that takes us to this place. Don't worry."

The last time she'd been able to get through to the highway patrol, the road wasn't open yet. That meant Lorenzo couldn't have gotten to Jenna—even if he had somehow found out where she was.

But still Rose couldn't relax. She knew how dangerous Lorenzo Dante was. With his connections, who knew what he was capable of?

She feared Franco had found out—just before he'd died. All attempts to contact him through the safe numbers she'd been given had proved fruitless. Her instincts told her he was dead, but she still held out hope that she was wrong.

The Jeep roared up the mountain through the trees, Mike deftly steering it around boulders and tree stumps from when the area had been logged.

She looked at the map. If she was right, they weren't that far from Fernhaven.

LORENZO COULDN'T SIT still. He paced the interrogation room, cussing cops. "How long can they hold me?" he demanded of his lawyer.

Anthony Cruise sat in the corner, a small man in a dark suit, with a pockmarked face and sharp features. "Depends on if they book you."

"They aren't going to book me," Lorenzo said confidently. "They're just trying to scare me. They haven't got anything on me."

His lawyer glanced at the mirrored wall as if to remind him that cops were probably behind it, watching the two of them.

Thank goodness he'd had the presence of mind to put Alfredo on Charlene before he'd opened the door to the cops, Lorenzo thought. All Alfredo had to do was follow her to Jenna and take care of things. Jenna had said she wanted to return his money, but he didn't trust her.

He thought of the duffel full of money as *his* now. If he could get to it before Valencia, he could take at least half and hide it. Let Valencia think Franco and Jenna had split the money. Made a lot more sense than the two of them being romantically involved.

Lorenzo thought he could sell a story that Franco and Jenna had hatched a plan to rip off the money and split it. Then Franco would meet up with his girlfriend, Rose Garcia.

Valencia might actually buy that. And Lorenzo would come out the winner on every count. Franco's body would never be found—or his half of the money, which was two hundred and fifty large.

But first Lorenzo had to get out of the police station.

When the door finally opened and the big cop, Detective Luke Henry, came in, Lorenzo snapped, "Charge me or let me go. I know my rights, dammit."

JENNA COULDN'T BELIEVE she'd had the dream again. She woke flushed, the robe sticking to her damp skin. She sat up, shocked to see that it was late. How long had she slept?

She swung her legs over the side of the couch and stumbled to her feet, disoriented and confused, the dream trying to drag her back.

Hurrying through the suite, she jerked open Lexi's bedroom door, afraid her daughter would be gone. The four-year-old was still snug in the bed, asleep in the dim light.

Jenna rubbed her arms against the instant chill. Once they got away from this hotel she would forget the man from the old photograph. Forget Harry Ballantine. He didn't exist except in her mind. In her dreams. She conjured him up in her need to be loved. And yet no man had ever felt so real.

Disoriented, she stood for a moment, just letting her heart rate come back down. What scared her was what the dream had left her with. It hadn't just been sex. Someone had made *love* to her.

And the dream had left her feeling safe…a dangerous thought. But nothing like the ones that came after it. The dream had left her feeling…loved. Cherished. Protected. Alive. Whole. Blessed.

She laughed at her own foolishness. What she was was crazy. Lorenzo had tried to push her over the edge, to drive her nuts, and now he'd succeeded.

She shook her head, clearing away those thoughts.

Charlene would be here soon.

Jenna had to get the money ready.

Then she would wake Lexi and they would leave with Charlene.

For now, Jenna closed the door to her daughter's room and padded barefoot to the living room. She picked up the phone and dialed the front desk.

"Elmer, I need a box and some tape for a package," she said.

"What size? I can scare up one and bring it to you," he said cheerfully.

She gave him the dimensions.

"I saw one in the kitchen that should work. By the way, the highway patrol called. Good news—they think they will have the road open soon."

"That is good news." Jenna hung up, telling herself that Lorenzo would be so happy to have his money back that he would leave her alone.

That once she and Lexi left here, they could put all this behind them.

She hurried into her bedroom to pack, but was drawn to the bathroom. The mirror had cleared, but the words were still there.

HARRY
BALLANTINE

She closed her eyes, willing away not only the letters, but the way he'd made her feel. Her body still tingled from his touch. She thought she could smell him in the small room, almost feel his breath on her neck.

Her eyes shot open. The scream caught in her throat.

Chapter Eleven

"Where are you?" Raymond Valencia demanded when Rico finally called in. "Do you still have Charlene Palmer in sight?"

"Stuck in traffic. And yeah, she's just a couple of cars ahead of me, stuck in the same roadblock. But the road is supposed to open soon. There's, like, a jungle on both sides of the road. Creepy, if you ask me."

"Where are you on the map?" Raymond snapped impatiently. He could hear Rico rustling the paper as he tried to get the map open.

Raymond tried to control his impatience. He feared he'd sent Rico on a wild-goose chase. And after hearing about the police taking Lorenzo down to the station, he feared Jenna might already be dead. Franco, too.

Rico finally gave him the road number and the

last town he'd been through. "I'm headed east, but according to the map there isn't anything up here but some place called—" more map rustling "—Fernhaven."

Fernhaven? It took Raymond a moment to remember where he'd heard that name before. A few months ago he'd received an invitation to the grand opening of the Fernhaven Hotel. It was a recently rebuilt hotel in the middle of nowhere, with some tragic history that dated back to the 1930s.

Could that be where Charlene Palmer was headed?

"No towns close?" he asked Rico.

"Nope."

First Charlene got a car she couldn't afford and now not only was she headed for a hotel she couldn't afford, but the place wasn't even open for business yet. Or was it? He felt better about sending Rico after her. Raymond would soon be finding out what Charlene was up to. Obviously she was doing something for Lorenzo. Maybe the car, the hotel, were her payoff, along with the apartment rent. Raymond could well imagine what her duties might have been, given that Jenna lived in the same apartment house.

He would take the chance that Charlene knew where Jenna was. Or at least what had happened to her.

Either way, Charlene Palmer wouldn't be returning to Seattle.

"You're sure of your location?"

Rico made a disgruntled sound, accompanied by what seemed to be an attempt to refold the map. "It looks like we're finally going to get under way. They're removing the barricades."

"Listen to me. I think I know where Charlene's headed. When you get to where she's going, park somewhere so you won't be noticed and call for me. I'll take the chopper. I don't want Charlene to see you, no matter what. Have you got that?"

"Got it," Rico said, in a tone that said he wasn't stupid.

Raymond wished he could believe that. "I'll be there within the hour." He hung up and called the pilot to get the helicopter ready.

ONCE FREE OF THE COPS, Lorenzo pulled out his new cell phone and called Alfredo. He answered on the first ring.

"What's going on?" Lorenzo demanded. "Don't you dare tell me you lost her."

"Nope, I can see her car up ahead. We're stopped because of some road problem. I tried to call you—"

"I had no cell phone for a while."

"She's got another tail, though. Picked it up right after we left the apartment. I've been following both her and the tail."

Lorenzo tried to calm himself. "Who else is following her?"

"Dunno. I'll take a look."

Lorenzo heard Alfredo's car door open, then close. He waited.

After a few minutes he heard the sound of the car door opening, the springs on the seat groaning, then, "Hey, can you believe it? It's Rico Santos."

Rico. Lorenzo swore. So Valencia was one step ahead of him. How? *Charlene.* Had she sold the information to Valencia? Lorenzo wouldn't put it past her. He swore again. "Tell me where you are." He took down the directions. "Did Rico see you?"

"Naw, I didn't think you'd want me letting him know I was following her, too."

"Good work, Alfredo. Now make sure Rico doesn't follow her any farther. When she reaches wherever she's headed, call me and wait for further instructions. I'm on my way."

He remembered that Jenna's car was still parked at the service entrance. The damn cops had turned the tow truck driver away so they could search her car. Lorenzo had told the cops that it had some kind of mechanical problem and that's why Jenna had left it there and called someone to give her a ride home. He didn't know who. He didn't care.

Now he would have to call the towing company again. They would charge him double. But he never wanted to see Jenna's car again. He should have dumped it in the lake the way he had Franco's.

He quickly packed his belongings. Charlene had promised to call as soon as she had the package. As if he would trust her to do that. A woman like Charlene would open the duffel—if Jenna was stupid enough to still have all that money in nothing more than a duffel bag.

From where Alfredo said he was stopped in traffic, it was a good two-hour drive. But Lorenzo had no choice but to head up there. Alfredo would buy him time by taking out Rico. And if need be, he'd have Alfredo take care of Charlene and get the money.

Jenna, though, was another story. As dangerous as it was, Lorenzo wanted to take care of her himself.

MY GOD, SHE COULD *SEE* HIM.

Jenna stumbled back, a look of horror on her face.

It's all right. Don't be afraid.

Harry didn't dare move toward her. He still couldn't believe that she could see him. He wanted to rejoice, to sing and dance and shout. *She could see him.*

"Please go away," she moaned as she backed up against the wall of the bathroom, then slid down to the floor, as if her legs would no longer hold her up. Tears welled in her eyes. She bit her lower lip and squeezed her eyes shut.

Is that really what you want? He stepped toward her, desperately wanting to touch her, to reassure her, to look into her eyes and have her gaze into his. He'd never dreamed this would ever happen. Not after seventy years of being nothing. Of not being heard. Or seen.

But now…

She tried to draw back as he cupped her cheek with his hand. "Please, don't." But even as she said the words, she turned her head to press her lips into his palm. Her tears splashed down over his fingers. He could feel them, just as he could feel her.

Somehow she had breached the barrier that had enclosed him all these years and kept him prisoner.

I don't know. I think you were sent here. For me,

he thought. This woman he felt such intense emotions for had opened a door and released him. And now the ache to live again was so strong in him that he knew he would do *anything* to reclaim a place in her world.

Open your eyes. Look at me.

MIKE FLANNIGAN SLAMMED on his brakes and swore.

Rose caught her breath as she stared at the cliff just feet in front of the Jeep. The logging road had ended without warning in a fifty-foot drop into a creek bed.

"I guess I should have taken the other road back there," Mike said as he carefully put the Jeep in Reverse and backed up.

Rose didn't let out the breath until they were far enough from the dropoff that she dared inhale again. Her hand went to her side.

"Are you feeling all right?" Mike asked.

She dropped her hand. She could feel the scar through the fabric of her shirt and realized that it had become a habit, touching it, almost as if it had become a reminder.

"The knife wound is healed. I'm fine."

"Right." Mike turned the Jeep around in a wide spot and started back up the road. "You really think you're up to taking on some really bad bad guys?"

"I'm just going to warn Jenna, that's all."

Mike chuckled. "Right. Lorenzo isn't already out on bail and tracking her, too. Probably hasn't sent any of his thugs after her, either." He shook his head and shot Rose a glance. "It isn't your fault she married him."

"People make mistakes," Rose said, remembering the young, gentle woman she'd met in the park. "Jenna made a big one. But she shouldn't have to pay with her life. Not to mention the price that little girl might have to pay."

Rose swallowed, willing back the tears that burned her eyes. She remembered Lexi from the park.

Mike seemed to let the silence lie between them for a moment. "You have a plan if Lorenzo and his gunmen show up?"

She had no plan. That wasn't like her. She preferred having a plan of action, if it was working on her house or working on a case. She was winging it and that alone should have scared her. "I'm going to get Jenna out of there before they can find her."

"There's something you should know," Mike said. "The word on the street is that a big payoff is missing. Raymond Valencia is looking for Franco. Lorenzo is somehow involved. But there is a fear that there will be retribution. If there hasn't already been."

Was this about a missing payoff? Or about Jenna?

Rose closed her eyes. "I just can't shake this feeling that Jenna is in worse trouble than even having her ex after her."

Chapter Twelve

Charlene Palmer had taken every precaution to make sure she wasn't followed. In the busy traffic around Seattle she hadn't spotted any car twice.

But once on the two-lane road heading east she kept seeing a large black car behind her. She figured Lorenzo would have her followed. She'd hoped she'd lost the tail before now. Maybe she hadn't.

She wasn't that worried. Even if it was one of Lorenzo's men, he wouldn't stop her until she had the package, and since she had a backup plan…

She'd locked the doors on her car while waiting for the road to open, and patrolmen to remove the barricades. There hadn't been but a handful of vehicles in line behind her, the black sedan one of them.

Now that they were moving again, she didn't

see the vehicle. Maybe it had turned off. Maybe it hadn't been following her at all.

She tried to relax. She had a nice car. Soon she would have twenty thousand dollars to go with it. Actually, more than that if her plan worked. And unless she missed her guess, she would no longer be needed to spy on Jenna Dante. She'd never liked doing it, anyway.

Wisps of fog began to drift across the highway. She'd been climbing for miles. Up here, the trees were thick on each side of the road, walls of green that hemmed in the highway. Around the next bend, the fog grew more dense. She caught a glimpse of black clouds shrouding the tops of the mountains. A storm was coming in. She liked storms.

She turned on her headlights and slowed as she checked her rearview mirror. There was one set of headlights a good distance behind her, but she quickly lost them in the fog and trees as the road snaked up the mountainside.

Glancing at the mileage gauge, she saw that she should be almost to Fernhaven.

And there her life would finally begin.

FEAR KEPT JENNA'S EYES squeezed tight. *Hurry, Charlene. I have to get out of here.*

Jenna tried to remain calm. Charlene would be here soon. By this time tomorrow Lorenzo would have his money back. She and Lexi would be on a flight to some country far from here. Everything would be all right. She would forget this place and what had happened....

Jenna.

She shook her head and put her hands over her ears. She heard him chuckle.

You know that won't do any good. Look at me.

She felt a sob escape her lips as she opened her eyes.

He was crouched next to her on the floor, looking exactly as he had in the old photographs downstairs. He wore a tuxedo, his dark hair oiled and combed back. His eyes were the most beautiful blue she'd ever seen. She felt a jolt as she looked into them.

He met her gaze.

Jenna's heart beat faster. It *had* been him in her dreams. She could see it in his eyes. He'd been here last night and again this afternoon. He'd made love to her. He'd made her believe that anything was possible. His touch had ignited a passion that had been missing in her life, and she didn't want to let it go. She wanted this phantom lover to come to her, to make love to her, to never ever go away.

As if he knew that, he reached out and pulled her into his arms, drawing her to her feet.

She closed her eyes, feeling tears well behind her lids as she leaned into him. He felt solid. Real. "What is going on?" she whispered.

"I'm not sure. This is as much of a surprise to me as it is to you."

She pulled away from him and stepped deeper into the room. "Who is Bobby John Chamberlain?" she asked, slipping her hand into her jacket pocket.

"Jenna—"

As she turned, she withdrew the gun from her pocket and pointed it at him. He seemed to shimmer in the light. Not a figment of her imagination. But not *real,* either.

Harry groaned and looked disappointed. "Put down the gun, Jenna."

"Who are you? *What* are you?" She gripped the weapon tighter.

He met her gaze. "You already know."

She shook her head. "No, I don't. Tell me I dreamed it."

"It isn't a dream," he said quietly.

She shook her head. "But this isn't possible."

"I don't know how or why, but you were sent here. Sent to me." He stepped toward her.

She raised the gun to point it at the spot where

his heart should have been. "I have to know who you are."

"My name *is* Harry Ballantine, and part of me has been waiting my whole life for you. Isn't that all you have to know?"

She shook her head once more.

"Jenna, let me help you. Put down the gun. It won't do you any good. You can't kill me. I'm already dead."

"No." She recoiled, her hands trembling so hard she almost dropped the weapon. She stumbled back, losing her balance.

He caught her, gently took it from her and eased her down onto the couch. Flipping on the safety, he put the gun on top of the television cabinet, out of Lexi's reach.

Jenna felt as if all was lost. She'd lost her mind. Worse, she'd lost something else—a part of herself—to Harry Ballantine. No matter who or what he was, a part of her would always remain here with him, whatever happened now.

"I'm sorry." It was all Harry could think to say. Because he was sorry in more ways than she could ever know.

She was shaking, her eyes glittering with tears. He didn't know how much time he had. She could still see him, but he didn't know for how long.

"You came here so I could help you," he said.

She shook her head yet again, her eyes wide as she stared at him. Her face had blanched white and he could see the fear. The disbelief. He'd been there and understood how hard it was to accept some of life's—and death's—little surprises.

"I think I knew the moment I saw you," he murmured. "You have to let me help you. It's the only way."

"Why should I believe anything you tell me?" she demanded, her voice breaking.

"Because a part of you knows how I feel about you," he stated. He could see her fighting it.

"I don't understand any of this," she said with a sob.

"Listen to me, Jenna." He gripped her hands. "I know you're in trouble. There are people after you."

She tried to pull free. "How can you know that?"

"The same way I know you were sent here. I feel it." He let go of her hands. "You're in grave danger."

Tears welled again in her eyes. She glanced toward the door to Lexi's bedroom. "I have to protect my daughter."

"I know. I'm not sure how, but I want to help you." He didn't tell her that he had a plan, and if it worked, they would be together—one way or another. Because he could never let her go now. They were meant to be together. Even if she would have to die to stay here with him.

The phone rang, startling Jenna. She'd completely forgotten about Charlene. She got up and went to answer it, her back to Harry.

"Hey, it's me," Charlene said. "I'm starting up the mountain to the hotel. Everything okay at your end?"

"Yes."

"You sure? You sound like someone has a gun to your head," Charlene stated, as if she might be only half joking.

"No, I'm fine. Just nervous. I want this over with," Jenna said.

"Hang in there. It will be over before you know it." Charlene disconnected.

Jenna wished she could believe that as she hung up the phone and turned.

Harry was gone.

She hadn't heard the door open. Nor close. She checked the rest of the suite. Gone. As she came back into the living area, she glanced quickly to the coffee table, where she'd put the taped-up cardboard box that she'd filled with money.

It was still there.

But part of her had expected it to be gone.

Chapter Thirteen

Lorenzo couldn't believe this gas-hog of a car he'd rented. He pulled into a fuel station at the edge of some Podunk town and happened to glance in his rearview mirror.

A dark-colored sedan swung to the side of the road in front of an abandoned store. Jolly. The son of a bitch was tailing him!

Lorenzo jumped as someone tapped on his side window. A kid in a grimy green uniform looked down at him. Lorenzo turned the key back on and hit the button that lowered his window a few inches.

"Fill 'er up," he said to the attendant as he realized he'd pulled into a full-service pump instead of a self-service. He hated to think what gas cost in a town this far from anything. A ghost town. Most of the storefronts were boarded up and there was no one on the street.

He looked into his mirror again. Jolly was still sitting in his car, waiting.

Lorenzo opened his door, got out and stretched, his back to Jolly. "Where's your restroom?" he asked the attendant as he walked around the front of the car.

The kid pointed to the back. "Key's just inside the door."

The key was attached to a carved piece of log that had to weigh two pounds. Lorenzo took it from the hook and carried the stupid thing around the side of the building, discarding it the moment he was out of sight.

He ran around back, sprinting across a side street and skirting the rear of the abandoned store, then up its side to the corner. He stopped to screw the silencer onto his gun, then keeping low, came up behind the dark sedan. Jolly was facing forward, watching the station, waiting for him to come out of the john.

The attendant at the gas station finished filling up Lorenzo's car, then sauntered back inside the station without even bothering to wash his windshield.

Lorenzo moved quickly forward, the gun against his leg. Once he was alongside, he raised the weapon and pumped three shots into the window.

The first shot shattered the glass. Nothing stopped the second and third ones from reaching their mark. Jolly slumped in the seat, eyes wide, mouth open.

Lorenzo went back the way he'd come, picked up the bathroom key and returned it to the office, hanging it on the nail where he'd found it. He paid cash for his gas, thanked the attendant, who hadn't even bothered to wash his damn windshield, and walked in a leisurely way to his car, all the time watching the street.

No movement of any kind. Especially from the dark car parked in front of the abandoned grocery store.

AT THE HELICOPTER PAD, Raymond Valencia tried Rico's number one more time before boarding. He hadn't been able to reach him. Either cell phones didn't work high in the Cascades, or something had happened to him.

"Where's Erik?" Raymond asked in surprise as he slid up into the seat of the small chopper. With some alarm, he saw that this man wasn't his usual pilot. The guy couldn't have been over thirty, with startling blue eyes and blondish hair that was too long and curled at the collar of his leather bomber jacket. He looked as if he belonged on a surfboard at the beach, not at the controls of a chopper.

"Flu bug. Your service called for a pilot." The guy gave him a look as if to say, "So here I am." He stuck out a big suntanned hand. "John James Harrison."

Raymond shook his hand, a little less uneasy when he felt the strength of the man's grip. There was also a confidence about the young man. It eased Raymond's mind some as he watched him ready the chopper.

"How long will it take to get there?" Raymond asked.

"Half an hour once we're off the ground."

"You been flying long?"

Harrison gave him an amused smile, showing a lot of white teeth as he cranked up the engine. "Since I was a kid. My father was a pilot," he said over the whoop-whoop of the blades.

Raymond nodded and tried to relax. Half an hour. He glanced at his watch, wondering what he was doing. This was a mistake. He should never have gotten involved in Jenna Dante's life to begin with. More to the point, Lorenzo Dante's life. Raymond hoped he was wrong, but couldn't help thinking he was somehow responsible for Jenna running. For her taking his money, if indeed she had. For what was bound to be a showdown at some remote hotel in the Cascades.

He'd always been so careful to stay in the shadows. Others before him had ended up in prison or dead because they got their hands dirty. They'd become public figures, with their photographs in the paper all the time depicted as crime bosses. He'd seen enough of those shots on the evening news to swear he wouldn't be one of them. He lived a secluded, quiet life and was very careful.

Now he'd broken his cardinal rule. He was getting involved. And for what? Five hundred grand? He knew it had little to do with the money, although half a million dollars wasn't anything to sneeze at.

He had to know who he could trust. That was much more important than money. He had to know who was behind this—and see that they were taken care of.

He felt his gun, where it was tucked in against his ribs. He hadn't killed anyone in years. Not that he hadn't kept up his marksmanship abilities at the shooting range he'd installed in the lower level of his home.

Some nights he shot round after round. He knew that to truly be safe, he needed to be able to protect himself. Then he would bowl in the single alley he'd had built next to the shooting range. No one knew about the bowling because he didn't want anyone to know just how lonely he was. Just how alone.

And that, he knew, was why he was doing this. Not because of the money or the trust issue. He wanted Jenna. He'd wanted her from the first time he'd laid eyes on her and he'd found out that Lorenzo had married the girl.

Raymond had been sick with desire for Lorenzo Dante's wife. And now he could have her. She would be grateful for his help. She would owe him. Especially if she'd taken his money. Even if she didn't want him, he knew he could convince her that she belonged with him. He would protect her. And her daughter. From Lorenzo.

The helicopter lifted off. The sinking sun glinted on the high-rises in downtown Seattle. The Space Needle stood alone, a soaring landmark, glowing in the sun.

The chopper headed east, crossing over miles of traffic-filled highways, clusters of small communities, until finally the landscape below them turned green.

Raymond breathed a sigh of relief, leaned back and closed his eyes. He thought about Jenna and prayed that she wasn't involved in trying to rip him off. Especially that she wasn't in this with Lorenzo. Raymond knew he couldn't forgive that.

Heavy at heart, he hated to think what he would have to do if he found out that Jenna had betrayed him.

CHARLENE CAME UP OVER THE rise and there it was. Fernhaven Hotel.

Even through the rain and fog, the place looked amazing.

"Wow." Charlene had dreamed about living a life like this. Fancy hotels, breakfast in bed, people to wait on her....

But how had Jenna Dante gone from that fleabag apartment where she'd lived to this? Last Charlene knew, Jenna had less money than Charlene herself.

Blackmail? Was she selling these so-called papers to her ex?

Charlene smiled at the thought. Would be nice to see Jenna get some backbone, that was for sure. The woman was more beaten down than Charlene had been even during the worse part of her marriage. Her husband used to kick her butt, but Charlene had always come back fighting.

She pulled into a spot in the parking lot near the

trees, where she figured her car wouldn't be that noticeable, and turned off the engine.

The rain seemed to fall harder, with gusts of wind blowing it sideways across the windshield. She debated waiting to see if it was going to let up. Yeah, right. She wished she'd thought to grab an umbrella. Or at least a rain jacket. But she'd been thinking of sunny beaches, because she had no intention of ever going back to Seattle unless it was to catch a plane to a warmer clime.

She sat for a minute just gawking at the hotel. Never in her life had she ever stayed at anything more than a cheap motel, let alone a place this fancy. Maybe after she got the package from Jenna, she'd stay the night. What would it hurt to make Lorenzo Dante wait?

She knew the answer to that one. But there was little that scared Charlene anymore. She'd seen the worst of it in other men like him. Nothing could scare her now. Not even Lorenzo. He could hurt her physically, kill her, make the last few minutes of her life pretty miserable, but in the end, he couldn't take anything else from her because she had nothing worth taking. Death would be a welcome relief.

Not that Charlene had any intention of dying anytime soon. Nope, she'd put away any money she came across. Hidden it. She had added to her nest egg with the money Lorenzo had been giving her to spy on Jenna.

And now she had a car and was about to add twenty grand to what she called her "freedom fund."

She was a lucky woman, she thought, as she waited for the rain to let up. She had overcome obstacles that would have killed most men. And with no education or a husband or many prospects, she'd found ways to take care of herself.

Not that she was proud of spying on Jenna. She liked the woman, related to her. But this was about survival. And Charlene Palmer was determined to survive—no matter what she had to do.

It was a lesson that Jenna Dante still had to learn.

"Picking up some wind," the pilot said as Raymond Valencia's helicopter neared the hotel. The chopper began to shake, buffeted by the gale. Fog rushed by, and suddenly rain splatted off the helicopter like bullets off bulletproof glass.

Through the rain and fog, Raymond Valencia caught a glimpse of Fernhaven and was instantly filled with an unexplainable dread. He'd read about the hotel being rebuilt on the same spot where *fifty-seven people* had died in 1936, after a fire had swept through the original hotel. This place was said to be identical.

A fierce cold seemed to envelop the helicopter. He shivered and looked over at the young pilot, wondering if it was only his imagination or if Harrison felt it, too.

Harrison was frowning, seemingly intent on flying the chopper, and having some difficulty.

"You should be able to put it down in the parking lot," Raymond said. Thunder cracked, so close he felt the hair stand up on the back of his neck. Right behind it came a loud boom.

The pilot had to yell to be heard over it. "No way are we putting this baby down up there. The chopper's too light for the kind of wind coming down off that mountain. It would be suicide to try to land up there."

"What do you think you're doing?" Raymond demanded when Harrison started to turn the chopper around and head back the way they'd come. Raymond could see the clearing. They were too close to turn back.

He pulled his gun from the holster and pointed it at Harrison. "Fly this chopper as if your life depended on it and take me to the hotel."

Harrison looked from Raymond to the gun in his hand and smiled, while still fighting to keep the chopper in the air. "I knew when I woke up this morning this wasn't going to be my day."

Raymond looked out. He couldn't see the lights of Fernhaven through the pouring rain. "You think I won't shoot you?"

There was a loud thunk and the engine sputtered. "Shooting me might be the kindest thing you can do right now," Harrison said as he fought the controls.

You're going to die. The thought seemed to come from outside Raymond as the chopper suddenly began to buck. Then the engine died and the craft rolled to the side, dropping toward the dense green forest below.

The trees came up fast through the rain and fog.

Raymond could hear the pilot on the radio. "Mayday, Mayday."

Raymond thought his life might pass before him. Instead his last thought before the chopper crashed was of his mother. At least she would mourn his death.

DARK CLOUDS HUNG OVER the hotel by the time Jenna saw a red car come up the mountainside and park at the back of the lot. It was raining so hard it was difficult to tell if it was Charlene. No one got out of the car.

Jenna waited, afraid. The wind groaned and raindrops ricocheted against the glass, obscuring her view.

What if it was Lorenzo?

Jenna held her breath as she stared down at the car, waiting to see who got out. Part of her was screaming, "Run! You can't trust anyone." Especially Harry Ballantine.

You can't trust anyone.

Especially your own instincts.

Or even your own eyes.

It was Harry's voice again in her head. She shivered, convinced she was losing her mind.

Even when she saw the figure finally emerge from the red car, for a split second her brain saw Lorenzo. She recoiled, then blinked. It was only Charlene. No one else got out.

Weak with relief, Jenna clutched the window frame and finally allowed herself to breathe. No one else was in sight as Charlene started through the rain toward the hotel entrance.

As a BOLT OF LIGHTNING split the dark sky, Charlene looked up at the hotel and almost died.

She barely heard the boom of thunder, followed in a heartbeat by an explosion that lit the sky.

While Charlene had always been a little bit

psychic, it wasn't like being a little bit pregnant. You had to work at the craft, hone your skills. Charlene had never liked work.

At an early age she'd accepted her so-called "gift," but also knew she didn't want to foresee her future.

"I don't have to be psychic to know it's going to be bad," she'd often said. "I'd rather be surprised than to see how bad it's going to be before I get there." So she'd pretty much learned to block it out.

That is, until the moment she looked up at Fernhaven, saw all the faces in the windows and knew that only one of the those looking down at her wasn't dead yet.

Her blood turned to slush. She no longer felt the rain pelting her. All she felt was fear gripping her by her throat.

Being a little clairvoyant, she should have known that a tragedy such as the one that had struck the original Fernhaven did more than scar the land. The horror stayed, trapped there often for eternity. Or until something or someone released the poor souls. But she now felt that truth to her very bones.

This place was haunted with the fifty-seven dead. Not only could she see and feel them, she knew enough to fear them. Fernhaven was a graveyard of lost souls and, she realized with a shudder, they'd been expecting her.

Chapter Fourteen

Harry sent a warning to Jenna, but knew he had to stop Charlene. She couldn't be trusted. He sensed it on some level he couldn't explain.

As Charlene started toward the steps of Fernhaven, he moved in front of her.

To his astonishment and regret, she walked right through him. He saw her shudder as if she felt something, but clearly she couldn't see him. Or feel him. Only Jenna and her daughter were aware of him.

Which meant he had no way to stop what was going to happen.

Then, to his surprise, Charlene turned and looked back. Not at him, but at the headlights coming up the road. She quickly stepped into the shadows and waited.

The car stopped at the edge of the trees. The lights went out, the engine suddenly silent.

Charlene moved through the cover of darkness toward the car.

Something shone for a moment in her hand as she neared the vehicle and the man sitting in it, trying to get his cell phone to work.

"Mr. Dante, if you get this message, it's Alfredo. I'm at that place, Fernhaven, waiting like you told me to." He snapped off the phone, grumbling under his breath.

The man didn't see Charlene coming, didn't hear her steal alongside the car. Not until it was too late.

AFTER JENNA SAW CHARLENE disappear from view, she hurriedly packed up and put her suitcase by the front door.

She checked on Lexi, only to find her glued to the television. Jenna didn't allow her daughter to watch much TV, so this was a treat for her. She felt she had failed Lexi in so many ways.

A mother protected her child. Even against the child's father. Jenna hadn't done that. Worse, she wasn't sure she could in the future.

She closed the door to the sound of Lexi's childish laughter and Fred's irritated meow. Lexi hadn't said any more about her father. Only that she wanted a "new" daddy, a nice daddy.

Hurry, Charlene, hurry.

When Jenna heard a soft knock, she ran to the door of the suite and threw it open, belatedly realizing she should have asked who it was first.

Charlene stood in the doorway, soaking wet and looking as if she'd aged. She was panting, her face ashen, as she burst into the room, motioning wildly for Jenna to close the door.

"Did someone follow you?" Jenna asked as she quickly closed and locked the door. "Lorenzo? Is he after you?"

Charlene seemed surprised by the question. She shook her head and, putting a hand to her breast, said between breaths, "It's not Lorenzo." She glanced around the suite, eyes widening.

"Are you all right?" Jenna had to ask. Her neighbor didn't look all right. For a moment Jenna wondered if Charlene was having a heart attack.

"I'm fine. Just…winded. Where's Lexi?"

"In the other room watching cartoons," Jenna said. "Thank you so much for driving up here. I really appreciate it."

Charlene nodded, her gaze going to the taped-up box sitting on the table. "That it?"

"Yes. I just need you to leave it in my apartment. I'll call Lorenzo and tell him where to pick it up once I know you made it home safely."

"Yeah. This place…" She waved a hand through the air and met Jenna's gaze. "It doesn't bother you?"

Bother her? Jenna wanted to laugh. This place made her crazy. "I'm anxious to leave, if that's what you mean. I'm all packed. I was hoping you could give me a ride to the nearest town."

Charlene was starting to breathe a little freer and didn't look quite so pale. She dragged a sleeve over her face and Jenna saw her shiver.

"I'm already packed," she repeated, motioning to her suitcase by the door. "I just need to get Lexi."

Charlene nodded.

"Are you sure you're all right?" Jenna asked her. "Would you like a glass of water?"

"No," she answered. "I'm fine. It's just the altitude up here. I'm not used to it."

Jenna smiled at her. "Thank you again for doing this. I owe you." She stepped to her daughter's door and opened it. "Time to go, baby."

"Go?" Lexi said from the bed. "No, Mommy."

Jenna turned off the TV. Lexi protested, burrowing down under the covers. Jenna picked up Fred. He began to protest, too.

She carried the cat and Lexi's suitcase into the living room and put the suitcase by the door next to her own. Charlene was standing at the window, looking out through the rain-streaked glass.

Jenna went back into the bedroom. "Lexi, please don't fight me. Not now. Baby, we have to leave. Don't you want to go on a big plane?"

Lexi peeked out from under the covers. She'd been crying, her face tearstained. It broke Jenna's heart. The child had been uprooted so much, and now Jenna was taking her away from the one place Lexi truly seemed happy.

"A really big plane," Jenna said, hearing the pain in her voice. She smiled, hoping to hide it from her daughter.

"Is Daddy going with us on the big plane?" Lexi asked.

Jenna could hear the fear in her daughter's voice. "No. He's not going with us."

Lexi pushed back the covers, scooped up Clarice and reached out to her mother. Jenna grasped her in her arms and headed for the living room. Reaching the bedroom doorway, she halted.

Charlene was standing near the front door. She had the box of Lorenzo's money under one arm. She held a gun in her free hand. The barrel was pointed at Jenna, and it had a silencer on the end.

"Give me Lexi," Charlene said in a voice Jenna scarcely recognized. "Give me the child. Don't make me force you."

"Charlene—"

"Now!" the woman snapped.

Lexi started crying. Jenna stepped back, thinking that if she could get into the bedroom and close and lock the door...

Charlene dropped the box and grabbed Lexi's arm before Jenna could carry out her plan. Struggling to hang on to her child, Jenna didn't see Charlene swing the gun in a deadly arc.

She felt the stunning blow, though, felt Charlene pry Lexi from her arms. And then Jenna was falling, screaming out her daughter's name as she pitched toward the darkness.

Lorenzo couldn't believe it. A hotel at the end of the road?

He stopped, furious at Jenna for bringing him to this backwoodsy place. He liked cities. Dark woods made him uncomfortable. Add one hell of a rainstorm and he wanted to ring her neck. And Charlene's, and even Alfredo's...

He took out his cell phone and called Alfredo. No service. Lorenzo had told the man to stay put, but as he drove by Alfredo's car, even in the dark he could see that Alfredo wasn't sitting inside, waiting. What was wrong with him?

A chill crept along the back of Lorenzo's neck. He rubbed at it with his hand as he realized Alfredo always did what he was told. He was too dumb to do anything else.

Something had happened.

Lorenzo looked out through the driving rain, considering what might be waiting for him at the hotel. Alfredo had killed Rico at the roadblock. Lorenzo had seen Rico's car pushed off to the side of the accident site.

And with Jolly out of the picture, who did that leave?

Jenna? Lorenzo scoffed at the idea. Sure, she'd taken the gun he had hidden in the bedroom, but did she even know how to use it? Unless she'd learned since divorcing him.

He ground his teeth at the thought of what his dear ex-wife had been up to since the divorce. But one thing he knew for certain: Jenna didn't have what it took to pull a trigger. Not to mention he was the father of her only child. No matter how she felt about him, Jenna couldn't kill him.

So that only left…Charlene. Lorenzo groaned as he shifted the car into Drive and parked at the edge of the lot—where, through the pouring rain, he could see the vehicle he'd bought Charlene. She would have his money by now. She would think she was going to live to spend it. Charlene didn't scare him. He'd kill her before she had a chance to do to him what she must have done to poor dumb Alfredo.

THUNDER CRACKED OVERHEAD, a boom that shook the Jeep.

"Well, I'll be damned," Mike said, and pointed through the rain.

Rose saw the lights, dim in the pouring rain. "That's got to be it." Fernhaven. She felt herself tense, afraid what they would find once they reached the hotel.

Maybe they should have waited for the road to open. It might have been faster. For all she knew Lorenzo could already be down there.

She checked her weapon in the shoulder holster beneath her jacket. Fully loaded. She had an extra clip in her pocket and a knife in her boot, a little trick she'd learned from Luke.

Glancing over, she saw the truth in Mike's gaze. He knew she hadn't come all this way just to warn Jenna. Ever since Jenna had confided in her about the horrible things Lorenzo had done, Rose had been determined to take the man down. She'd hoped that she could do it legally—by getting Jenna to turn state's evidence against Lorenzo.

That had failed. Then Rose had been injured on another case.

Now she had a chance to make sure that Lorenzo Dante never hurt another person.

Mike reached over and squeezed her knee. Their eyes met in silent understanding. He understood her need to right wrongs—even if he didn't agree with it. But they both knew that things could go very wrong once they reached the hotel. "Be careful," he said.

She nodded. "You, too."

He smiled and shifted the Jeep as they dropped off the mountain, down what had once been a logging road but was now little more than a trail. With luck it would come out fairly close to the hotel.

Rose could see the lavish building through the rain and fog. She felt a chill, remembering the ad she'd seen announcing the opening of Fernhaven. The owners had touted the hotel's former elegance, its hot pools, its ornate, detailed decor and the big draw: its ghosts.

"MOMMY! I WANT MY MOMMY," Lexi cried as Charlene half carried, half dragged her down the hallway toward the elevators.

"Shut up!" Charlene snapped, stopping to shake the little girl. "Listen to me. You ever want to see your mommy again, you have to shut up. You understand?"

"I don't like you," Lexi said, choking on her sobs.

"Well, I'm wild about you, kid," Charlene said sarcastically. "I'll tell you what. If you quit crying and come with me without any more trouble, I'll give you some candy. Chocolate. You like chocolate, don't you?"

Lexi turned to look back down the hall. "You hurt my mommy."

"No, she just fell down. She'll be fine once she rests a little. We'll get some chocolate out of my car and then we'll see if she's ready to go with us, how would that be?"

The kid was giving her a suspicious look. Lexi had always been too bright for her own good.

Lexi had to run to keep up as Charlene half dragged her down the hall. The box under her arm was a lot heavier than it looked. *Papers, my behind.* There was something good in this box, something Lorenzo Dante would pay anything for. Charlene would bet on that.

But just to even the odds, there was always dear little Alexandria as a bargaining chip if Lorenzo tried to cheat Charlene out of what she had coming. She was no fool. She liked having all the odds on her side.

They reached the elevator and she pushed the button. She could feel the spirits. She jabbed at the elevator button. *Come on.*

Lexi was waving at someone down the opposite hall from where they'd just come—an odd bat in a purple hat with feathers. No one better try to help Lexi or stop Charlene.

The elevator doors opened and Charlene lurched in, jerking Lexi after her. She punched the close button three times before the doors shut. Then she leaned against the wall, breathing hard. Nervous sweat poured into her eyes. She wiped it with her sleeve.

Just a few more minutes and she would be out of this place. She looked across the elevator. She couldn't see them now, but she knew they were there watching her. The arm holding the heavy box began to tremble. She wanted to put it down but she couldn't. She leaned against the elevator wall, chilled and sweating, fighting for her next breath.

The elevator stopped. The doors opened. Charlene practically dived out, dragging Lexi with her.

The lobby was just yards away. She could see

the door that opened onto the wide porch. Once she was through it…

LORENZO LOOKED AROUND, surprised to realize the hotel didn't even look open for business. There was only one old pickup parked across the lot, other than Charlene's red car and Alfredo's vehicle back in the trees.

Odd. Was it possible Jenna wasn't even here?

No. Charlene had gotten a call from her. Charlene wouldn't try to double-cross him until she got her twenty grand. The woman was a lot of things, but she wasn't that stupid.

But what could Jenna be doing here?

He knew the smartest thing would be to wait in his car for Charlene. She'd eventually come back out with the money, and when she did, he'd be waiting.

But not only did he hate waiting, he couldn't stand the thought that Jenna had to be close by. What if she somehow got away?

During the whole trip up here he'd been imagining the look on her face when she saw him. He smiled to himself, enjoying the terror he would see there. Killing her was going to make all this worthwhile.

Then he would take Alexandria. The thought

didn't please him as much as he'd imagined it would. Before, he'd known that Jenna would suffer, knowing he had their daughter. But if she was dead…

He realized he was having second thoughts about taking Alexandria with him when he left the country. If she'd been a boy, a male heir, it would be different. But he had a feeling she would be more trouble than she was worth.

And she was a strange child. He'd seen her studying him sometimes, and there were moments when he thought she could see beyond his veneer, see things he didn't want anyone seeing.

Yes, the more he thought about it, the more he didn't think he would take her. After all, she'd probably grow up to give him as much grief as her mother had. Maybe he'd just leave her here. She was cute enough that someone might want her.

He glanced toward the hotel.

Where the hell was Charlene?

He couldn't wait any longer. He'd just started to open his door when a Jeep came roaring up to the front door.

Lorenzo couldn't believe his eyes as Rose Garcia jumped out and ran toward the lobby of the hotel, followed by the man who'd been driving.

What the hell was she doing here? And who

was the guy? Hell, they both looked like cops, now that he thought about it.

He quietly closed his car door and slid down in the seat. This wasn't going anything like he'd planned, and it was starting to make him very angry.

"Lexi?"

The child jerked free as a woman Charlene had never seen came running in the front door.

Charlene tried to grab the little brat, but realized it was futile. Lexi ran to the woman, crying again, saying, "She hurt my mommy."

Charlene shifted the box to get to her gun as she continued to run for the front door. Out of the corner of her eye she saw Lexi launch herself into the woman's arms. Who the hell was that?

As she reached the front door she saw a man coming in. She fired at him when she saw him going for a weapon. He dived to his right, but she saw him clutch his side, grimacing in pain. She'd shot him!

She was hit with a blast of cold, wet air, then was out the door, across the porch and heading down the steps.

She didn't look back, couldn't. She ran as if she was running for her life. She was.

Once she reached the pavement of the parking

lot, she looked over her shoulder. She saw the man limp inside, the front door of Fernhaven closing behind him. No one chased after her. She'd gotten away.

Charlene slowed, breathing so hard she couldn't hear over her gasps. She'd never moved that fast in her life. She laughed. She didn't even notice the rain.

Because of the storm, an odd darkness had settled over the landscape, creeping her out almost as much as the hotel had. She half ran, half walked toward her car. The box was so heavy, and she was still having trouble catching her breath, especially at this altitude. She was used to sea level. She was also in terrible shape.

She wasn't even sure who she was running from anymore. She'd seen things back there in that hotel that she never wanted to see again. Felt things that would haunt her until the day she died.

But at least she would have money. More than twenty grand.

She'd parked near the edge of the lot, thinking to hide her car beside the dense vegetation. Now she wished she'd parked right at the front door.

A damp, cold breeze stirred the trees and bushes, with a rustle like a hoarse whisper. Dark shadows moved in and out, in sync with her frightened breaths. As Charlene moved away from the lights of the hotel, she felt as if she were falling into blackness.

She slowed to rest for an instant. The air felt heavy. The dark clouds low. She labored to breathe, straining to hear over the clamor of her pulse.

Through the pouring rain she thought she glimpsed another vehicle parked near Alfredo's in the trees. She was almost to her own car when she heard it.

The scrape of a shoe sole on the parking lot pavement.

She didn't turn—just ran, lumbering toward the little red car, the nicest thing she'd ever owned.

She never reached the car.

He hit her from behind.

She fell forward, unable to break her fall because of the box in her hands. She went down hard, landing on the box, which knocked the air out of her.

Charlene rolled over on her back and looked up. At first he was only a large black shadow. No features. No real shape. Just a faceless monster in the dark.

"You stupid bitch."

Still gasping for breath, she pushed herself up

into a sitting position as he began to take shape before her eyes. Lorenzo. She'd know that voice and that attitude anywhere.

"I tried to call you," she said.

It was the wrong thing to say, and she knew it the instant the words were out of her mouth.

He kicked her in the thigh, the pain excruciating. Charlene let out a howl and bent over her leg.

He was on her then, grabbing a handful of her hair and snapping her head back so she was forced to look into his face. The face of the devil.

"Shut up or I'll cut your throat," he growled between gritted teeth as he knelt beside her.

The knife glittered in his hand, and she didn't doubt for a moment that he meant every word. She endured the pain, biting down on her lip.

He wanted something, needed something from her, or he would have already killed her.

"Where is Jenna?" he asked, tightening his hold on her hair, making her gasp back another cry of pain.

"Room 318. I got your package for you." Charlene tried to look at the box on the pavement, but he jerked her head up so she had to gaze at him.

He raised the knife blade so she could see it.

As he held her down, he reached over and drew the box to him. Carefully he slipped the blade beneath the tape and sliced. The top flapped open and he reached inside.

"What the hell?" He waved something in front of her face. "What is *this?*"

She could only stare as he dumped the contents of the box on her chest—brochures advertising the new Fernhaven Hotel. These were the papers that were so important to Lorenzo that Jenna had gotten Charlene to come all the way up here?

"Where is my money?" Lorenzo demanded from between clenched teeth. *"Where?"* He slapped the brochures away in a wild gesture, then put the knife to her throat.

"I don't know. I swear. She told me there were important papers in the box."

Lorenzo's gaze seemed to harden to stone. "The two of you were in on this, weren't you? You are going to regret it till your last breath."

An odd icy calm washed over Charlene. She looked at Lorenzo, seeing all the men who had used and abused her, men she'd allowed to hurt her in ways she couldn't bear to remember. Or forget.

And now another man wanted to take pleasure in her pain.

"You're too late," she said, and smiled up at him. "Jenna's gone, and so is your kid *and* your money."

Lorenzo reacted to her words just as she knew he would, and for the first time in her rotten existence Charlene Palmer really was free.

Chapter Fifteen

Jenna. Jenna. He's coming!

She stirred, head aching. "Harry?"

Thank God you're okay.

She blinked and looked around the room, her blood running cold. "Lexi! Where's Lexi?"

She's all right. She's with a cop and a private investigator downstairs. She's safe.

Jenna slumped against the wall in relief. "The police are here?"

Who is Lorenzo Dante?

"My ex-husband," she said, fear turning her stomach.

He's here. Get the gun I put on top of the TV cabinet.

"Where are you?" she asked, looking around the room. "I want to see you."

"I'm here."

She watched him materialize just a few feet away from her, and felt such a surge of emotion to see him again.

"I'm powerless against him, Jenna. You're the only one who can see me. Feel me."

She nodded, feeling just as powerless against Lorenzo.

"There is something else I need to tell you."

She pushed herself to her feet and had to stop for a moment as her vision dimmed and her head swam.

"It's about the money that was in the duffel bag."

"Charlene took it," she said, and couldn't believe that she'd trusted that woman. It just showed how bad her instincts were. Like now. She looked at Harry. She saw the expression on his face. "No."

"I switched the boxes."

She let out a laugh and shook her head in astonishment. What part of "he's a thief" didn't she get?

"You have to understand. I thought I would spend the rest of eternity here, feeling nothing, being nothing. But then you came and changed everything. I want to be with you, Jenna. I can't stand the thought that when you leave here, I will go back to being nothing again."

"What did you think you were going to do with the money?" Out of the corner of her eye she saw that the suite door stood open. she took a couple of steps toward it.

He grabbed her arm. "It was just an old reflex and this crazy hope that I could buy my way out of here. That I could be with you. I thought with something this strong between us, maybe…"

She looked into his eyes again and realized what he was saying. She felt tears fill her own eyes as he pulled her to him. In his arms, she had believed anything was possible, but now she realized only one of them would be able to leave here. No amount of money could buy Harry Ballantine's way out of Fernhaven.

"He's just outside, Jenna." Harry released her and went to the TV cabinet. He picked up her gun and handed it to her.

She took it, her fingers trembling. She still felt light-headed, and her heart was so filled with regret that the gun felt extra heavy in her hands.

Can you kill him? He'd asked the words in her head.

She met Harry's gaze. He must have seen that instant of hesitation. She heard him groan.

"We're going to need another plan. Quick, come with me."

FOG DRIFTED PAST on a light breeze as Lorenzo cautiously approached the hotel.

Jenna couldn't have gotten away. Charlene had to be lying. He wiped a smear of her blood from his knuckles onto his pants, wondering what she'd done with his money.

What nagged at him was that Charlene had looked as surprised as he'd been when the money hadn't been in the box.

He slowed. The afternoon was dark, the clouds low and heavy with moisture. Mist moved through the air like floating cobwebs, and a strange cold feeling seemed to settle in his bones.

A light glowed in the lobby, and in front of it he saw figures in the lobby—Rose Garcia and the man she'd arrived with.

Apparently the man had been shot, because Rose was helping him. Alexandria was with her.

Lorenzo swore as he watched them disappear from view. He didn't need any more trouble. All he wanted was his money. And Jenna.

Staying in the shadows, he moved up the steps and across the wide porch. No sign of Rose and the man. Where had they gone? He drew his gun and eased open the front door. The place was eerily empty. The lush, thick carpet muffled his footfalls as he moved quickly to the registration desk and quietly checked the book.

The first guest since 1936 was a Jenna Johnson. Johnson? Yeah, right. According to the book, she was in room 318. So Charlene at least hadn't lied about that. All the cubbyholes behind the desk contained two keys, except for the slot marked 318. It had only one in it.

He pocketed the key with a smile and turned toward the elevator.

As he did he heard a sound coming from behind the door marked Manager. He heard Rose Garcia calling the police. Too late to stop her. He'd just have to move quickly and finish his business here before the cops arrived.

At the elevator, he pushed the button and waited. He was considering taking the stairs instead when the elevator doors opened and he saw an elderly, gray-haired man. The man's surprised gaze went from Lorenzo's face to the gun in his hand.

Lorenzo stepped in, the elevator doors closing behind him as he reached over and hit the third-floor button.

"Who the—" That's all the old man got out before Lorenzo backhanded him with the gun. The old man slid slowly to the floor as the elevator hummed upward.

LOCKED INSIDE THE MANAGER'S office, Rose worked to stop Mike's bleeding. She'd pulled off her jacket and folded the soft fabric, pressing it against the gunshot wound. Mike was pale, his skin clammy.

"A lot of help *I* was to you," he said.

She smiled at him. "You're just a high-priced private eye. You're not used to women shooting at you. Or are you?"

His smile was feeble. "I didn't see the gun in her hand until it was too late. I was looking at you and Lexi."

That's what she'd feared.

Lexi was crying softly. Rose pulled her closer. "It's all right." She met Mike's gaze. "I've called for backup and an ambulance."

He nodded and covered her hand with his. Their eyes met and she felt her heart drop like a stone. "Don't dare think about taking off on me," she murmured. They both knew what she meant.

"Not a chance," he whispered. "Not after I finally got you to admit you wanted to date me."

She looked at Lexi. Where was the little girl's mother? Was Jenna still alive?

"Go on," he said. "Find Jenna. I'll be all right. I'll take care of Lexi."

He looked as if he might pass out at any moment. Rose knew if she left him he might die. She glanced from Mike to the little girl. Lexi had curled up beside Mike, hugging her rag doll and looking terrified.

"I know what you came up here to do," Mike said quietly.

Kill Lorenzo, Rose thought.

"Go ahead. I wasn't going to try to stop you," Mike said.

She felt the pull. She was a cop. A cop on medical leave. Out of her jurisdiction. On a mission. She *had* come up here to make sure Lorenzo Dante was stopped for good, and Mike knew it.

"Several of the highway patrol are close by because of more flooding on the road," she said.

She could hear sirens in the distance. They would be here soon.

"I'll be all right," he whispered.

She shook her head. She couldn't leave this scared little girl alone with a man who might bleed to death while she was gone. "The highway patrol will find Jenna and help her." If Jenna was still alive.

Rose looked into Mike's eyes. She had thought she would do anything to stop Lorenzo Dante. But she was wrong. "I'm not leaving you," she whispered. "Or Lexi. Come here, sweetheart," she said to the little girl. Rose might not be able to help Jenna right now, but she could protect her daughter. "Everything is going to be all right."

Lexi moved into the circle of Rose's arm as the three huddled in the dim office, the sirens growing louder and louder.

HARRY DREW HER DOWN the hallway. Jenna heard the elevator begin to rise three floors below. She looked up at the dial over the closed doors. Someone was coming up. Lorenzo?

The stairs. Take the stairs!

She looked around for the door to the stairway. Harry grabbed her hand and they ran down the hallway as the elevator dinged behind them. They were still yards away when the elevator opened.

Harry pulled Jenna into one of the rooms that wasn't quite finished yet.

She tried to hold her breath as she heard the heavy tread of footfalls on the hall carpet. The elevator doors closed. Silence. Then she heard the door to suite 318 bang open. She looked over at Harry. He motioned for her to wait.

She looked into his eyes—bottomless blue eyes. She tried to imagine living in the same time he had, being with him then, and her heart ached.

She thought about opening night at Fernhaven, June 12, 1936.

Closing her eyes, she imagined being in the big ballroom with Harry, dancing to the music of the orchestra. She could almost smell all the flowers she'd seen on the tables, their scents mixing with the expensive perfumes the women were wearing.

Jenna would be dressed in a gown the color of Harry's eyes. He would hold her close and they would sway to the music. She could almost feel his heart beating next to hers to the old-fashioned strains…. Then she heard the sound of breaking glass, and Lorenzo swearing.

LORENZO STARED DOWN at the broken lamp on the floor, then looked around for something else he could destroy. If Jenna was hiding in here, he'd find her.

He still had the gun in his hand, but he wasn't going to shoot her. He thought he might choke the life out of her so he could watch her die. He wanted to be the last thing she saw when she left this earth.

He couldn't believe this was where she'd been staying. A suite? The bitch had been staying in this elegant place on his money?

He moved deeper into the suite to check in the closets, under the bed. He'd seen her suitcases by the door. If she'd left, she'd left everything behind. Just taken the money, he thought with fury.

That's when he heard the creak of door hinges down the hallway, and swung around. The stairs. He could hear her footfalls on the steps.

JENNA RAN DOWN THE STAIRS, practically throwing herself down the stairwell. It was cold and gray in here, and her footfalls echoed loudly.

She couldn't hear if Lorenzo was behind her, if he was gaining on her. Nor could she hear or see Harry. Was he still with her?

Then she heard the door bang open above her, heard Lorenzo's lumbering steps, as if he was half falling down the stairs in his rush to catch her.

Breathe.

Her heart thundered in her ears, louder than the horrible sound of Lorenzo gaining on her. And she felt an overwhelming sense of relief that Harry was still with her.

Then, suddenly, there was the exit door. Ground floor.

Take that door.

She shoved it open and stumbled out into the

stormy darkness, met by a wave of cold dampness.
It took her a moment to realize where she was. The
courtyard. The only light was around the fountain.
Everywhere else held pockets of shadow and mist.

Run to the path up the mountain.

"Harry?"

Run. You have to trust me.

Trust him? She could hear Lorenzo coming
down the stairs.

Wait.

She had reached the edge of the courtyard,
where the dense forest began.

Wait for him.

She stopped. "Harry, you're scaring me."

*I'm going to help you. But you have to trust me.
Can you do that, Jenna?*

She took a deep breath and let it out.

Mist rose from the hot pools as Jenna waited at
the edge of the courtyard for Lorenzo, wondering
what she was doing. More to the point, what Harry
was planning.

*Let him see you, then take the path behind you.
Trust me.*

She let out a small laugh, half-hysterical, at the
sound of Harry's voice in her head. She'd more
than lost her mind. She was about to lose her
life. At least Lexi was safe. She did trust that

Harry had told her the truth about her daughter. She could hear the sound of sirens growing closer.

There he is.

She could feel the gun tucked at the small of her back. Through the steam rising off the hot pools she saw Lorenzo come out the door into the courtyard. He spotted her and smiled as he began walking toward her.

This was crazy. But Harry was right about one thing. It had to end on this mountain. Jenna couldn't live in fear the rst of her life. She had to protect her daughter.

She turned and started up the path, through the dense woods, as Harry had instructed. As she climbed, following the narrow track, the trees like a wall on each side of her, the clouds grew darker, the fog thicker. She could barely see two feet in front of her.

She didn't look back, just kept climbing. Lorenzo wasn't worried about catching her. His arrogance wouldn't allow him to hurry. He thought he had her right where he wanted her. Maybe he did. Maybe this voice inside her head was of her own making. If so, then Lorenzo had driven her to this.

We're almost there.

The sound of Harry's voice sent a stab of yearning through her. She hadn't lost her mind. Instead, she'd found something else here at Fernhaven. Something she couldn't bear to lose.

She slowed as the path reached a small clearing. Mist swirled around large boulders and wind-twisted trunks of cedar trees.

Walk just ahead and wait for him. Stop.

Jenna stared back the way they'd come. A breeze stirred the tops of the trees, swirling the fog and mist, making a low groaning sound. The air was cold and damp and seemed to cut through her clothing. She hugged herself to still her trembling as she caught a glimpse of something moving through the fog toward her. Lorenzo?

She drew the gun and started to take a step back, but Harry stopped her.

There's a cliff behind you.

Jenna swung around. She could see nothing but fog. She kicked a small rock and heard it drop over the side, hit way below her, then again, the sound echoing up until she heard nothing. She could feel Harry with her.

Jenna...

She turned back around, hearing something in Harry's voice that scared her more than standing on the edge of a cliff.

"What is it?"

We're not alone. I don't know who it is.

She heard a strange sound in his voice and began to shake harder as a figure slowly took shape out of the mist.

Raymond Valencia stopped just yards from her. He looked odd, his clothing almost too neat after the climb up the mountain.

"Raymond?" Why did she get the feeling it wasn't really him? "What are you doing here?"

"He can't save you, Jenna," Raymond said. "He was never interested in saving you—only himself. He's a con man, Jenna. A thief. Haven't you realized that?"

Who was Raymond talking about? Lorenzo?

"He tricked you, Jenna. Made you fall in love with him. You think it's a coincidence you ended up at Fernhaven?" He shook his head. "He willed you here, knowing you were in trouble."

She shook her own head. "I don't know what you're talking about."

"Harry Ballantine, Jenna. He's the one who got you here so you could save *his* life."

She stared at Raymond, her heart in her throat. Raymond Valencia knew about Harry?

"Tell her, Harry. You stole Bobby John Chamberlain's identity so you could attend the Fernhaven grand opening to steal the jewelry you knew would be here. But you got caught in the fire. Except Bobby John Chamberlain was supposed to die. Not you. Not Harry Ballantine. Come on out, Harry. Show yourself. Don't be shy."

"How do you know all this?" Jenna cried.

"Because Raymond Valencia's dead, Jenna," Harry said, materializing beside her. "His helicopter crashed not far from here in the storm."

"That's right, Jenna," Raymond said. "I can't help you, either. But I can warn you. Harry wins either way. If he fails, he's trapped here for eternity. But then so are you."

She felt her knees go weak. None of this was happening. She was still inside the hotel on the floor, suffering from a concussion after Charlene had hit her. Maybe she was dead. Or maybe just dreaming.

"There is no redemption for Harry Ballantine because of the life he led before his untimely death," Raymond said. "No matter what he does, he isn't leaving this place. Save yourself, Jenna, before it's too late."

Redemption? Is that what this was about? The mist seemed to engulf Raymond. Jenna stared at the spot where he'd been standing, but he was gone.

She looked over at Harry. Their eyes met. Was it true? Was he nothing but a thief and a con man? Had he lured her here for his own reasons? "Tell me what he said isn't true."

His image seemed to fade. He said nothing.

She heard the snap of a twig, the scuff of a shoe on stone. Lorenzo came lumbering up over the rise. He looked winded and his pants were muddy, as if he'd fallen.

He leaned against one of the large rocks, obviously trying to catch his breath, but his eyes were on her. His lips turned up in a smile. "Looks like it's just you and me, Jenna. You shouldn't have taken my money."

Jenna took a step toward him, remembering the cliff behind her. Lorenzo had strength and size on his side, not to mention a weapon under his jacket. Lorenzo always had a weapon close by.

He pushed himself off the huge rock he'd been leaning on and sauntered toward her. "You didn't really think you could get away from me, did you?"

"No," she said, realizing she never had. "I guess I always knew this moment would come."

He was close enough that she could smell him, the sweat, the blood, the stale, leftover fear. "This is some freaky place you picked to hide in, you know?"

If he only knew. She drew the gun from behind her and pointed it at his heart.

He froze in midstep. "What do you think you're doing?" He let out a coarse laugh. "You don't even know how to use a gun."

She fired off a shot that ricocheted off the rocks behind him.

He swallowed, his face going slack, a flicker of fear showing in his eyes. "So you learned how to fire a gun. You ever see a bullet rip through flesh? Ever see someone die right before your eyes? It's an ugly sight, Jenna, one you would never get out of your head." His smile broadened. "Firing a shot into the air is one thing. But put a bullet into a man? The man who fathered your daughter? The man who you once loved?"

He started to step closer.

"Don't!" Jenna cried, her finger tensing on the trigger. He was right about one thing. She couldn't shoot him.

She lowered the gun, dropping it to her feet as she braced herself.

She'd already decided there was only one thing she could do: grab him and take him with her over the edge of the cliff. She tried not to think about leaving Lexi behind, because that would make her weak, and right now Jenna had to be strong. Dying herself was one thing, but she couldn't leave Lorenzo free. Couldn't leave knowing he could get her baby girl.

Lorenzo smiled. "I knew you couldn't shoot me."

She thought about what Raymond had said—that Harry had brought her here. That if he couldn't find a way to leave, then he would make sure she didn't, either. Was that why he'd brought her up here? He wanted her to die and be trapped here with him?

After you grab him, drop down and let the momentum of his motion propel him over your head and out.

At first she wasn't even sure she'd heard Harry, let alone heard him correctly.

Raymond's right, I can't save you. All I can do is try to help you. If you should fall, try to stay close to the edge of the cliff. There's a ledge about ten feet below you.

A ledge ten feet down. Right. "Always a con man, huh?"

Lorenzo frowned at her words. *"What?"* He quickly glanced behind him. "Who are you talking to?"

Jenna, Raymond was wrong, though, about us. If it makes any difference, I didn't bring you here. You were sent to me. I thought it was because we were supposed to be together. I guess I was wrong about that. Something is happening to me. Hurry. I feel as if I don't have much time.

"I asked you who you were talking to," Lorenzo snapped, and stuck his face into hers.

She grabbed him by the jacket and did as Harry told her, jerking him hard and at the same time ducking down. Her shoulder caught him in the groin. He let out a howl. His larger, heavier body went airborne over the top of her.

She'd done it!

Then she felt his fingers clutch the back of her jacket and find purchase. She was jerked backward. She grabbed at the ground, but the weight of his body pulled her over the edge of the cliff.

She turned in the air, throwing herself into the movement, breaking Lorenzo's hold on her as she shoved him away, propelling him outward and her toward the cliff.

But now she was falling, and below there was nothing but fog and the sound of Lorenzo's screams.

Jenna saw the ledge coming up at the very last moment. She closed her eyes, bracing herself for the inevitable. She hit, but something—someone—broke her fall.

She lay stone still for a moment, trying to catch her breath. Below her, Lorenzo's screams stopped with a sickening thud.

She closed her eyes and told herself it was over. She was alive. Lexi was safe. They would never have to fear Lorenzo again. "Harry?"

No answer.

Tears welled behind her closed lids. A sob escaped her lips and she choked on her tears. She had won. But her loss was overwhelming.

"Will I ever see you again?" she asked in a whisper.

She tried to feel his presence, but could sense him slipping away. She choked back more tears. "Do you have to stay here?"

Still no answer.

In the distance she could hear sirens and voices calling out for her.

But inside her head there was nothing but silence.

Chapter Sixteen

Jenna remembered little of the rest of that afternoon and night. Fernhaven had been crawling with police. There were dozens of questions, statements to be made, bodies to identify.

Only one memory would remain from the moment Jenna was lifted off the rock ledge and taken back to the hotel.

That image was the sight of her daughter running out of the back of the hotel and across the courtyard to meet her.

Jenna had fallen to her knees, throwing open her arms as Lexi ran into them. She'd crushed her daughter to her breast, crying tears of joy. They were alive. They had survived.

Lorenzo Dante was dead, his body broken at the bottom of the cliff. Raymond Valencia's body had been found along with the ruins of his helicopter, which had gone down in the storm not a half mile from Fernhaven.

Detective Rose Garcia had ridden down the mountain in the ambulance with P.I. Mike Flannigan. He was listed in stable condition. Word was he would recover. Security guard Elmer Thompson had suffered a slight concussion, but would recuperate.

Four other bodies had been found. Rico Santos was discovered dead in his car back down the highway. Rico, a known criminal, had been murdered in what looked like a professional hit.

Farther down the road, Gene "Jolly" Barker was also found murdered in his car. Same MO.

Charlene Palmer, wife of criminal Stan Palmer, had been stabbed to death in the hotel parking lot.

Alfredo Jones was also found dead in his car—shot at close range.

If she could have, Jenna would have left as soon as the police were through questioning her. But she had to wait until a rental car arrived from the nearest town.

The hotel provided everyone with rooms. Jenna asked for one on ground level. She couldn't bear to stay in room 318, knowing that was where Harry Ballantine, aka Bobby John Chamberlain, had died.

She put an exhausted Lexi down to sleep. "Can we go to the ocean now?" Lexi asked before she drifted off.

"Yes."

"Is Daddy gone?" Lexi asked quietly.

Jenna had told her that Lorenzo had an accident and was killed. "Yes, honey, he's gone."

Lexi looked sad. "Is he gone because I wanted a new daddy?"

Jenna hugged her daughter to her. "No, baby. He's gone because he couldn't love us enough. You and me, we deserve someone who loves us…bigger than the sky."

Lexi laughed and looked up into her mother's face. "Bigger than the sky?"

Jenna nodded, fighting tears.

The events of the past few days didn't seem to have scarred her daughter in the least. But Lexi had youth on her side, and what to her was a happy ending. All the bad guys were dead or in jail. Jenna and Lexi were both safe.

Jenna was just glad her daughter realized they had to leave.

As Jenna curled up on the bed, she prayed Harry would come to her in her sleep.

He didn't.

THE NEXT MORNING the hotel was still buzzing with police and crime-scene investigators.

Jenna loaded the suitcases into the rental SUV, checked to make sure Lexi had buckled herself in to the car seat, and put Fred next to her.

Then she slid behind the wheel. As she started the car, she glanced at Fernhaven. In the morning sun, mist bathed the rooftops, the mountain behind the hotel shimmered a verdant green and Fernhaven looked like a fairy princess's castle.

She hurriedly looked away, turning the SUV around and heading off the mountainside. She didn't look back. She couldn't.

"Hey!"

Jenna glanced in her side mirror and saw a man who'd been talking to one of the policemen. He waved to her to stop. She braked and lowered her window as he ran up to her side of the car.

"Hi," he said, and smiled.

He wore jeans, boots and a leather bomber jacket, and he had a knapsack thrown over his shoulder.

Jenna stared up at him. There was something familiar about the man. The smooth, self-confident way he moved. The set of his broad shoulders. Something so familiar, and yet she knew she had never seen the man before in her life.

"Any chance of hitching a ride out of here?" he asked.

"Sure."

His hair was a tawny blond, long at the neck, curling up over his collar. His smile broadened as he crouched next to the car so she didn't have to look up. His eyes were a clear deep blue.

"I kind of got stranded up here," he said. He glanced in the back seat and gave Lexi a wink. "It's the strangest thing. If I told you how I got here, you wouldn't believe it."

She looked into his eyes and saw something that lifted her heart like helium. Was it possible? "Where are you headed?" she asked. If Fernhaven had taught her anything, it was that there were things beyond earthly understanding.

"Don't really have a destination in mind, to tell you the truth." He laughed, the sound making Jenna's pulse quicken with a familiar excitement.

She glanced back at her daughter. Lexi was smiling at the man in a way that made her heart jump.

"We're going to the ocean," Lexi said excitedly. "Aren't we, Mommy?"

"Yes, we are," Jenna said. That was exactly where they were going.

"No kiddin'? I grew up on the California coast. You headed that far south?"

"Quite possibly," she said, surprising herself, scaring herself, and yet having never felt so right about anything.

He laughed again, wiped his right hand on his jeans and stuck it in the window. "John James Harrison. My friends call me Harrison."

Jenna's hand trembled a little as she shook his hand. It was large and warm and fit hers perfectly. "Jenna…McDonald. This is my daughter, Lexi, and the cat is Fred."

"Glad to meet you and I appreciate the ride," he said as he ran around to open the door and slide in. He smelled of the outdoors, a mixture of fresh air and green trees. "I'm planning to keep both feet on the ground for a while."

"Oh?" Jenna asked as she got the car moving again.

"I'm a helicopter pilot," he said as he settled in, putting the knapsack on the floor between the bucket seats. "My last job just about killed me."

"Really?" Jenna said, thinking about the chopper crash that had killed Raymond Valencia. This man had been the pilot? And he'd walked away without a scratch?

"Someone must have been watching out for me up there," he said, looking out the windshield to the blue sky overhead. "I thought for sure I was a goner. That was one close call. Something like that changes you. I know it sounds corny, but I feel as if I've been given a second chance. Silly, huh?"

Jenna shook her head, thinking of Harry Ballantine and second chances. "No, that's a feeling I'm pretty familiar with," she said and smiled over at the man beside her.

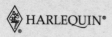

HARLEQUIN®
INTRIGUE®

The mantle of mystery beckons you to enter the...

MISTS OF FERNHAVEN

Remote and shrouded in secrecy—our new **ECLIPSE** trilogy by three of your favorite Harlequin Intrigue authors will have you shivering with fear and...the delightful, sensually charged atmosphere of the deep forest. Do you dare to enter?

WHEN TWILIGHT COMES
B.J. DANIELS
October 2005

THE EDGE OF ETERNITY
AMANDA STEVENS
November 2005

THE AMULET
JOANNA WAYNE
December 2005

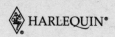
HARLEQUIN®

INTRIGUE®

As the summer comes to a close, things really begin to heat up as Harlequin Intrigue presents…

Big Sky Bounty Hunters: No man's a match for these Montana tough guys…but a woman's another story.

Don't miss this brand-new series from some of your favorite authors!

GOING TO EXTREMES
BY AMANDA STEVENS
August 2005

BULLSEYE
BY JESSICA ANDERSEN
September 2005

WARRIOR SPIRIT
BY CASSIE MILES
October 2005

FORBIDDEN CAPTOR
BY JULIE MILLER
November 2005

RILEY'S RETRIBUTION
BY RUTH GLICK,
writing as Rebecca York
December 2005

Available at your favorite retail outlet.
www.eHarlequin.com

HIBSBH

SPECIAL EDITION™

presents

the first book in a heartwarming
new series by

Kristin Hardy

Because there's
no place like home
for the holidays…

WHERE THERE'S SMOKE

(November 2005, SE#1720)

*Sloane Hillyard took a very personal interest in her
work inventing fire safety equipment—after all, her
firefighter brother had died in the line of duty. And
when Boston fire captain Nick Trask signed up to
test her inventions, things got even more personal…
their mutual attraction set off alarms. But could
Sloane trust her heart to a man who risked his
life and limb day in and day out?*

Available November 2005 at your favorite retail outlet.

Where love comes alive™